moving water

moving water

A NOVEL BY

JOAN SKOGAN

Porcepic Books
an imprint of

Beach Holme Publishing
Vancouver

This book is published by Beach Holme Publishing, #226—2040 West 12th Ave., Vancouver, BC, V6J 2G2. This is a Porcepic Book.

We acknowledge the generous assistance of The Canada Council and the BC Ministry of Small Business, Tourism and Culture.

THE CANADA COUNCIL | LE CONSEIL DES ARTS
FOR THE ARTS | DU CANADA
SINCE 1957 | DEPUIS 1957

Editor: Joy Gugeler
Production and Design: Teresa Bubela

Cover Photograph: Photograph of the Strait of Georgia where it meets the Fraser River by Rick Blacklaws. Used with permission.

Canadian Cataloguing in Publication Data:

Skogan, Joan, 1945-
  Moving water

"A Porcépic Book."
ISBN 0-88878-386-8

I. Title.
PS8587.K58M68 1998   C813'.54   C98-910854-6
PR9199.3.S543M68 1998

For Beatrix Mary Macintyre

Contents

...the sea, the unimaginable Pacific...no matter what you did to its edges, the true Pacific stayed inviolate and integrated or assumed the ugliness at any stage into some more general truth.

— Thomas Pynchon, *The Crying of Lot 49*

Freshes, the name given to the fresh water draining off the land after a period of heavy rain. Freshes increase the flow of the ebb tide as it recedes from the estuaries and mouths of large rivers, carrying land silt a considerable distance out to sea. In earlier times, freshes were a useful navigation aid, indicating the ship was off the mouth of a large river.

— *The Oxford Companion to Ships and the Sea*

On Roberson Point

*M*oving water changes everything it finds. Granite coasts, in time, soften under rainwash, rivers and the sea. River valleys spread, slackening their early v-shaped lines. Hillsides dissolve when sheet-floodwater from snowmelt or rain percolates down to their underground streams. "Landslip" is the geographer's word for this fallen earth. The repeated urging of salt or sweet water rounds the sharpest-edged stones, then absorbs their grains. Static hard matter can be held and carried within fluids constantly reconciling its form. Sand bars in the surf zone suspend themselves in seawater to shift longshore and cross-shore, eroding beaches and sending the sea further inland. A river scours its beds and banks for sand, silt and rock to carry as a wash load, fragments of quiescent mountains and deserts altered into motion. Whether sediment or boulders, the weight of land a river bears and bleeds into a swallowing sea depends on the ground, slope and seasonally shifting levels of its streamflow.

Yearly, fifty million tons of mud enter the Mediterranean Sea with the Nile. The hulls of cargo ships lying in Alexandria Harbour are clouded with the infused earth of Ethiopia and the Sudan. Rocky Mountain gravel rests almost three kilometres deep into the Pacific sea floor. The Fraser and Columbia rivers rise and receive most of their waters in the Canadian Rockies. These rivers drain another 400,000 square kilometres of mountain ranges and plateaus in British Columbia, Idaho and Washington State before they cede themselves to the Pacific on either side of the Canada/U.S. border. Along with other north-west coast streams and their tributaries, the Fraser and Columbia dump their wash loads onto the Juan de Fuca Plate. The accumulated weight of moved mountains forces deeper layers of the Plate at the bottom of the ocean basin to solidify into sedimentary rock. Until they are changed beyond recognition themselves, rivers change their findings. The Fraser and Columbia freshwater plume dilutes Pacific salt a hundred sea miles offshore.

Oceans answer with their own revisions wherever they find wide-mouthed river passage to push saltwater and tide inland. Estuary, from the Latin aestus meaning boiling of the sea, or tide. Spring tides on the Thames rise nearly seven metres at London. The Atlantic Ocean in the Gulf of St. Lawrence drowns the mouth of the St. Lawrence River, which widens from 13 to 113 kilometres at Anticosti Island. Tide affects the Skeena's feeder streams far inland from the port of Prince Rupert on the B.C. north coast.

There is nothing to be done about the tide except to know its power, taking comfort in its predictable intransigence. Tide, from the Saxon tid for time. For what might as well be forever— 300 million years in the Pacific Ocean, 200 million years in the Atlantic—seawater has risen, paused at slack tide, and begun to fall, twice a lunar day. The reaching swell of seas drawn to *the gravitational pull of the moon follows the lunar circle around the turning world, moving in and out, up and down, pushing and pulling, bringing and taking uprooted trees, planks of broken boats, pencilled notes in vodka bottles and jetsam—goods thrown overboard to lighten a sinking ship—onto the shore, or out to sea. Sometimes the sea sends back, changed, that which was lost. But little from the land returns entirely the same from the sea.*

Moving water must be the first memory. The earth, and our bodies, too, belong to water. Tissues of the flesh, living and dead, and of the soul, absorb water as they drift in a current that will, in a while, dissolve them into itself. We bleed and sweat and weep salt solutions similar to seawater. The pericardium, a sac around the heart of mammals, is filled with salty liquid moving in a small, contained tidal rhythm with every pulse. Moving water must be the first memory. Before birth, we roll contentedly on our own sea. Faintly salted water within a membranous sac in the womb moves as the mother's body moves, shifts its form to shelter the creature it contains. The unborn child swallows, absorbs and excretes the amniotic fluid while drifting at ease on its currents. When the waters break around us and pour away, we begin another passage. The first sea is almost forgotten. Its revenant mark on us remains in the water lapping in the bathtub, in the dreams and memories that rise, unbidden, on board a vessel moving on offshore ocean swells, and in the long watch for the tide.

Rose kneels to look at the body on the schist slab at high-tide mark, then lies down beside it on the stone. Her left hand, made into a fist, reaches out to touch the rain and seawater pooled in the upturned palm next to her. Now, Rose Bachmann, formerly Rose Bachmann Bruce, also known as Wild Rose and sometimes Rosamunde, Rose of the World, pokes the green rubber hood of her rain gear onto her head, and slides across the wet stone to complete her return to the north coast of British Columbia. Face up to the washed grey October sea of the sky, she sets herself into the carved form of *The Man Who Fell From Heaven,* the life-sized intaglio petroglyph on Roberson Point off the north side of Venn Passage in Prince Rupert Harbour.

The Man Who Fell From Heaven has lain here no one knows how long, on these dark rocks at the edge of the harbour around the corner from Metlakatla, where Tsimshian people and their ancestors have lived for at least four thousand years. His arms are outstretched. His parted legs end in splayed feet. Because the highest winter tides wash into him, his head and body hollows hold shallow, rain-rippled seas.

In summer, when more visitors come to Roberson Point, the places where the petroglyph man's eyes might have been are sometimes covered with quarters, nickels and dimes. In all her visits here before (during the other, still-married time), Rose never touched these coins, or added to their number or troubled to wonder if the sea or children took them away. She knew the stone body's water-filled cavities were never meant to be make-believe wishing wells the first time Richard brought her here to *The Man Who Fell From Heaven*. "You'll like this," he said, but he waited in the yellow skiff, shouting, "Further up," and "Look on your right," while she scrambled over the rocks. He never stepped ashore on Roberson Point when Rose knew him.

Years of her intermittent petroglyph pilgrimages went by before she remembered that coins on a corpse's eyes, and sometimes under the tongue, started out as money for Charon, the ferryman, to row souls across the Styx to the province of the dead. Better not to disturb those coins, or add to them and encourage that one-way river crossing.

Rose accompanies her every step with stories made from scraps of half-remembered history and myth, gossip, dreams and songs, but the man petroglyph is supposed to know only two tales. Tsimshian oral history says that long ago, likely when the clans were first making themselves known, a man of high position told everyone in his village he was going to heaven. Then he went away. This village was probably Metlakatla. Rose, lying in her open sarcophagus on the beach at midday, is certain that everyone in Metlakatla, a sea mile or two along the Pass, is eating a late breakfast, or lunch—probably clam fritters—right this minute, while wondering whether to get the afternoon boat into Prince Rupert or have another coffee.

The petroglyph man could have lived in any one of half a dozen other ancient Tsimshian winter village sites in Prince Rupert Harbour. These places still hold buried stone tools and shining abalone shell eyes on owl-headed clubs—such smooth, heavy assurance in the hand—and bone needles, as well as fragments of bodies once laid tenderly in cedar grave boxes before receiving amulets against the dark.

Everyone who made or used or mourned these things must have moved to Metlakatla, or up the Skeena River at salmon time, or made mythic journeys to the western isles—Avalon, Atlantis and others—and found them where the water turns shallow blue-green over the sands at Naikun, the Long Nose—sometimes called Rose Spit—on Haida Gwaii, the Queen Charlotte Islands. Or else everyone in the villages went to heaven themselves, leaving the rhythms of their lives beating silent, concentric circles in the air around their old homes.

Rose's fourteen years away from the north coast are nothing to the time stone mortars and mauls and their stories have lasted. Keeping watch with the petroglyph man until the tide falls another five and a half hours to low slack is only a moment in stone time. Even while she's shoving a cold hand under her sweater to loosen a too-tight bra so she can rest in a rock bed, Rose knows this. She still contains the charts she imagined when Prince Rupert Harbour, the Skeena River opening itself to Chatham Sound southeast of the city and the sharp-edged coast down to Cape Caution were new to her. The bearings on these interior charts are marked with material goods and stories left behind by the people in the old Tsimshian villages.

For a while after the coast, when other parts of the world fail to replace adamant cliffs and green, secret inlets, Rose will realize the encouragement she was given by the presence of stone bowls and spindle whorls known to have been held firmly in the hands of men and women working long tasks. Fragments of women's knuckle and finger bones, trenched with muscle tracks from weaving cedar strands watertight, comforted Rose more than she knew when she stumbled up Skeena feeder streams in late fall, counting spawned-out coho salmon with a clicker; or crouched on a forklift pallet high in the canned salmon warehouse for hours, picking tins for the Department of Fisheries and Oceans' Fish Inspection division. Consolation, faint and unrecognized then, of the company of bones, creeks, bears, stone bowls and copper bracelets who knew their own stories, continued to wash over her when she sat at a desk in the Prince Rupert Fisheries office.

Years after the Fisheries contracts and Richard, Rose, sitting on the floor in a library smelling of damp tea leaves and dust in another country, will find the words of a Siberian Chukchi man, recorded early in the century:

All that exists lives. The lamp walks around. The walls of the house have voices of their own. Even the chamber-vessel has a separate land and house. The skins sleeping in the bags talk at night. The antlers lying on the tombs arise at night and walk in procession around the mounds, while the deceased get up and visit the living.

This happens just across the water on the Chukchi Peninsula, Rose will think when she reads this, satisfied that she knows where she is in the world. But she means across the Bering Strait northeast of Prince Rupert.

In that library on the other side of the world, she will, for a moment, be Rose in the Fisheries office in Prince

Rupert on the north Pacific coast again. There she knew the nearness of stone containers, bones, and waters with lives of their own, even while she made notes on urgent demands for more fish from trollers, seiners, gillnetters, longliners, trawlers, tribal councils, sport fishers and owners of marinas, fishing lodges and processing companies.

An enlarged photograph of two bone needles from the back of a burial cave near Port Simpson kept company with her while she fumbled to form images from intricate lines of thread or ink in her workroom at home in Prince Rupert. The needles, looking still sharp, lying together in a bird-form basalt case as if poised to attend to long tasks, waited with her, watching the rain-slashed window instead of the work in her hands, for Richard Bruce to come home from salmon or herring fishing, or at least to call.

Rose used to take clouded, unacknowledged comfort, too, from stone pieces whose form and meaning changed, doubled back, shifted again—bears and halibut became humans on clubs with handles that were nipples, then phalluses; bowls that began as seals, then slid to become vulvas. The forms sometimes repeated themselves until mouths swallowed their own bodies. Shape-shifting and shadows, so taken for granted that tool makers attached them to everyday utensils, contented Rose, even in the up-the-coast years when she and Richard and everyone else still thought she would never be wild and dark or deliberately hidden. She was a sometime Department of Fisheries worker and a part-time artist, married to a fisherman. But she was also secretly, silently pleased when Raven emerged from the head of a man on a hammer, and when the open container of a double-designed paint dish acted as a mouth for the upper face, then changed itself into a belly for the body on its underside.

Change was not encouraged in the house on Arbutus Street in Vancouver where Rose grew up. Exceptions were made for Rose's father's experiments with pale blue as well as white dress shirts, and for her mother's suggestions that Rose become a less scrawny, more obliging child; then a prettier, not so dreamy girl; and then a smarter-looking young woman, with a life plan.

Arrangements on Arbutus Street were intended to be permanent. The sideboard crammed with cellophane-wrapped Bachmann silver, the heavy mahogany table with subordinate thin-legged chairs, the curtains partly closed even in daylight and the tightly tucked beds stayed in the same places forever, along with framed engravings of cities spiked with church spires, and villages set in hills too gentle to belong to British Columbia. Even innocent needle-worked footstools never abandoned their designated posts on the carpets. Flowers bloomed and wilted only outdoors, unless they entered the house as buds to be banished when they spilled pollen or petals. Rose's expansion from one shoe size to the next, and the rapid fraying of her scheduled short-back-and-sides haircuts were greeted with sighs.

"I'm growing my hair," announced Rose, "into braids," when she was nine, and, "like Janis Joplin," when she was sixteen.

"No, you are not," said one or the other or both parents,

which turned out to be true.

When Rose was a wife, the hair the colour of an old penny was an ally at last, vagrant as needed—pinned on top of her head in a knot of curls; pulled back into a tail moving in the wind, or loosened into a wild, wide tangle, for shelter.

In the married time, when Richard, smelling of diesel and salt, and once with a silver scale still stuck to his eyelid, came home from the boat to their bed, he would catch the mass of his wife's rust coloured hair into his fists to signal her to turn over or onto her belly or move toward him. Afterward, he muttered, "Rose, Rose, wild Rose," and sometimes, with infinite gentleness, mouthed the tendrils of hair straying in the hollow at the back of her neck.

But even when he was murmuring beside her in the bed, she wondered, some nights, about the promise of two Tsimshian stone masks made to fit snugly inside each other, as halves of a single work. Together, the masks are a basalt, sightless man's face, meant to transform, instantly, to another open-eyed, green stone version of himself. They must miss each other, those selves, Rose thought. The mask of the blind man from Kitkatla lives now in the National Museum in Ottawa. The mask with open eyes was taken from Metlakatla in 1869 to Musée de l'Homme in Paris with his willow mouth loop still tooth-marked. It never occurred to her, then, to tell Richard about the separated inward and outward gazing masks, or even to confess to herself how they disturbed her sleep some nights.

Rose, as an occasional and not-always-paid sketch maker for another museum in Prince Rupert, once held a small four-figured slate carving found on the beach across the harbour from the grain elevator. Its label said, "Of unknown purpose." The upper curve of a split-image killer whale contained a human centre whose arms became tail flukes, then perhaps bird wings, cradling an open-mouthed animal. All of these creatures fit sweetly round in her palm, and on the drawing paper. The figures transformed themselves into a crab without a shell when Rose held the little stone at eye level to look at it sideways, but the three handworked holes through the centre of the stone stayed a mystery for months. An old woman from the *Alaska Princess* stood in the museum one day, trembling with shy urgency, and asked the curator to let her touch that shape-changing pierced icon. Sometimes she could feel things. Not always, only sometimes. Kneeling before the commercial fishing exhibit mural, painting pre-1930s sail gillnet boats loaded low in the water with Skeena sockeye and spring salmon, Rose listened.

Silence for two minutes. Three. "Something about the weather," the cruise ship woman murmured. She'd seen a rocky beach and a woman standing with the double-sided stone raised to her mouth, blowing through the centre holes to change the wind.

Rose wondered if the wind-changer would still work. She could still hear the knife-edge of her mother's voice, "If the wind changes now your sulky face will stay that way forever." And Jean next door on Arbutus Street said, "March winds are bad for girls' complexions. March winds and May sun make clothes white, and maids dun." Richard hated whistling on the boat in case of whistling up a wind.

She abandoned the painted gillnetters picking up their nets, and took out her own sketchbook to draw a woman on a rocky beach with the weather charm at her mouth, raised to the sky. In Rose's sketch, the little stone carving released a stream of wind running narrow and fast around the woman, ready to bear her out to sea.

She might still have this drawing, not here in the early afternoon light on Roberson Point, but in one of the (after all this time) still unpacked boxes that will have to be shipped up to Prince Rupert now. The wind woman sketch could even be somewhere in the duffle bag full of paper in the trunk of the car parked at New Floats across the harbour. But right now, yawning and stretching until her boots are crammed into the stone-ridged feet of *The Man Who Fell From Heaven*, Rose is thinking only of the petroglyph man who would have lived in a world where weather charms functioned along with fish weirs, blades strong enough to shape stone, braided cedar-bark rope and other useful gear. He would have exiled himself from people whose lives Rose imagines as having contained a predictable measure of order and warmth.

Remembering her own hands in seawater at a temperature barely above six degrees centigrade most of the year between McInnes Light in Milbanke Sound and Langara Point just under the Alaska border; remembering setting a foot wrong in Skeena feeder streams and tributaries, so her hip waders filled with water while rocks rose from their river places to batter her ribs and slam the salmon fry traps out of her hands; remembering the weight of boots and wet clothes multiplied by long hours, and the wrist-dragging ache of forever still more dog salmon sliding off the gutting line the summer she tried being a cannery worker, Rose knows living could never have been easy here. Still, her imagined memories of a far, First People's past say: There was a place for everyone's feet in the warm ashes at the edge of the fire.

Then, the petroglyph man would have had familiar bodies around him, within his reach. Steamed halibut and salmon and the slippery, convoluted flesh of clams must have filled mouths and bellies with sea-tasting heat. Seal and deer bones would be sucked smooth, and the marrows cracked to leave lips and fingers gleaming with greasy satisfaction.

The air would have smelled of wood smoke and fog, and in late summer, of sun-warmed spruce and cedar, then heat-split salal berries. The trees: *amabilis*, called the lovely fir for perfuming the air and for firewood; Sitka spruce whose sharp needles protect dancers from evil thoughts, and whose roots make watertight hats and baskets; yew, called the bow tree by Robin Hood and the Haida; red and yellow cedar trees of life, entangled with salal bushes, lady ferns, bracken, devil's club and blackberries growing down to river banks and beaches, would have looked, then, as if they would last forever. Winter *halait* ceremonies when shamans invoked heavenly and animal spirit powers into form; spring moons called "everything sprouting"; and summer into fall river returns of sockeye, spring, coho, humpback and dog salmon must have seemed as if they could be counted on every year.

Rose assumes that darkness, or the fear of it, swelled somewhere in those lives, in pain and loss and untimely death or maybe at the back of the burial caves, and in the whirlpools near Aristazabal Island where Foam Woman devoured canoes and men. But a song or a prayer, a charm or a dance or a shaman's direction could keep you from wandering alone forever in the empty dark beyond the firelight.

So, the petroglyph man must have announced quite suddenly, Rose supposes, that he was breaking out of a circle of light and warmth. He was ashamed to stay, she believes. Ashamed of a contrary desire, even a need, to be alone in a world where survival required communion. She's certain now that *The Man Who Fell From Heaven* went away because he knew that neither he, nor anyone else in his village, not even the shaman's shadowface puppets with their water mirrors, could give meaning to the dry black emptiness he had come to contain.

The people from the village would have been his wives and children, his brothers, cousins, hunting partners, childhood friends and elders. They laughed when he said he was going away to heaven. Their laughter is always mentioned at the beginning of this first story about the petroglyph man.

So he disappeared. Not into the thick fir, spruce and cedar across the harbour in Tuck Inlet where the booming grounds are now, where there used to be bone beads on the beach. Not under the wild crab apple trees marking once-cleared ground near Shawatlan Creek and the Prince Rupert water reservoir. Not to sleep in the light of day with rainwet bracken ferns curved like cradling arms around his body, nor to rest anywhere on Canadian Hydrographic Services Marine Chart 3957, *Approaches to Prince Rupert Harbour*.

The petroglyph man didn't disappear into the places where you can wait, unseen, for the tide to change, watching seiners, fish packers and tugs going home through the Pass; where you can smell the city's smoke and see the pale spark of its day lights against winter-grey water and sky; where ships with names like *Anangel Might* or *Sealand Freedom* are loading grain, coal, pulp and logs; where coffee and cinnamon buns as big as a baby's head, heavy with carmelized brown sugar syrup, raisins and vanilla icing, are being consumed in offices and restaurants on Second and Third Avenues, as well as in the C.N. train yard and along the waterfront from Seal Cove to the Alaska Ferry Terminal; where beer drinking is beginning now, after eleven in the morning, opening time at the Belmont, Oceanview and Rupert Hotel beer parlours, as well as at the bar in the Crest, where scotch is served more often, and land otters can still sometimes be seen below the left front window, playing on the slippery float where the Port Simpson passenger launch ties up.

Rose will be aware that these ordinary acts are taking place now in the city across the harbour, along with other practices as likely to provide pleasure or practical result, even while she is anchored in her own port of refuge, nearby but hidden and unsought.

Port of refuge, as defined in Fishing Vessel Policy No. 12-93-15091: ...the adventures and perils...are of the seas...men of war, fire, theft, enemies, rovers, thieves, jettisons...surprisals, takings at sea...and of all other perils, losses and misfortunes, that have or shall come to the hurt, detriment, or damage of the said ship...and provided...the vessel...be at sea, or in distress, or at a port of refuge....

Rose will also know that love is being made, even this early in the day, by the people from whom she has separated herself. They will be practising forms of love in bleach-scented, faintly damp beds above the beer parlours; and at the docks, on old, or new and not-yet-paid-off work boats where men in engine rooms are bending over to tap her gently, to adjust her belts, or grease her shafts with a delicate touch, all to coax her—the Gardner, or Cummins or Detroit diesel engine—into giving a little more for a little longer. Love is under construction, too, at Port Edward out on the Skeena River slough, and in other places in the city of Prince Rupert: at lunch tables where children are laughing at grown-ups who don't know Sapporo Ichiban and Mr. Noodles need to be crunched in the package to break them up before you boil them; and in the bedrooms of old wooden houses overlooking a dozen sets of salmonberry and cedar-twisted stairs down to the harbour, rooms in which the one who sleeps alone, afterward, takes comfort from the slightly roughened texture of dried, salt-tasting stains on the sheets.

But the petroglyph man didn't hide himself in these harbour places, separated from familiar bodies and their affinity with one another. He went to heaven, and back. He insisted on this when he returned to his village one day, no one knows how long afterward. People laughed again. Rose can't decide whether the petroglyph man persuaded and cajoled, or shouted angrily, to get the people from the village to accompany him to Roberson Point where he showed them the shape in the rock marking his fall from heaven.

The second tale still told about the life-sized petroglyph says it marks the site where someone drowned and was tide-washed onto the rock to lie face up with the rain falling into open eyes, someone cherished enough in life to cause a stone body to be made in memoriam.

Now a fine light rain falls into Rose's own open eyes. She closes them, licks the drops clinging to her mouth, tastes sweet plain rain mixed with lip gloss. Oil and water. Glossy Fudge petroleum distillate. Rose figures she must have lost at least twenty, maybe more, pots of it somewhere along the north coast and in offshore waters. The tiny covered dishes flat enough to fit deep in her pockets, fell out, Rose guesses, while she was counting, catching, sketching or photographing fish, or just riding around on seiners, gill-netters, trollers, Fisheries patrol boats, foreign stern trawling ships, domestic draggers and seaplanes. Her lip gloss was sometimes forgotten from purses spending time on the ledge under the washroom mirror in cafés and bars in Rupert, Masset, Skidegate, Namu, Stewart, and upriver towns. It was given away once in a while to other women who needed colour, and retrieved, usually, from men who just wanted to look.

In Rose's experience, men loved lip gloss, the gestures, perhaps, as much as the results—the appearance out of your pocket as if it were a quarter or a pocketknife; the unscrewing of the lid to reveal a sticky circle never regarded with even a glance. Rose kept her eyes all the while on the sea off the bow, or on the guitar player on stage in the bar, or on the Fisheries papers lying on the conference table. Then, the delicate middle-fingered dabbing in the pot, and soft, absent-minded patting of moist colour onto the mouth. No mirror. No mirror and public application is the point of lip gloss.

Right now, the small plastic circle of gloss in Rose's pocket is jamming her hipbone against the rim of the petroglyph. She shifts, sighs, checks the still-falling tide, and rounds her back a little to settle more deeply into the stone. Rain still sprays softly from a light southeast wind, but she's keeping warm in the rain gear and a heavy roll-necked sweater whose secret name is the Black Russian, after the man whose gift it was, and because this sweater is saved for emergencies of the spirit as much as the weather. Her gumboots splay out to follow the feet of the drowned figure. She's dry enough except for the trickle of rain, and probably seawater, leaking along her neck, turning her hair into seaweed-brown strands tangled around her fingers when she fumbles with the soaked mass and the gaping hood. This is the rain gear design flaw—too loose a hood in the prone position. But how many lie down in the rain and discover this? Rose wonders.

She's drifting now. If she were going to add herself in this setting to the *Women in Glass Vessels* art collection she wants to assemble, she would mould *The Man Who Fell From Heaven* in black resin, very small, about fifteen centimetres, then form her own body from wired bones, probably gull bones she could find right here on Roberson Point. The bone assembly would be wrapped in minute scraps of salt-bleached cloth. There was an RCMP notice up for almost a year once, in the Alert Bay post office:

Unidentified body found drowned on the beach at Bull Harbour. Female, forty to fifty years old; probably Native origin. Fragments of blue-flowered dress.

She would sacrifice the old glass Japanese net float, first seen laden with forty years of barnacles, riding the Pacific two hundred sea miles offshore, scooped on deck by the crew of the black cod boat *Anne Sonora*. They gave the huge green globe to Rose, even though she wasn't the one who saw it first, even though she was only the Fisheries observer.

Rose can already list the acts she will perform to create a watery green world out of glass. She'll take the precious float from its position on the workroom shelf, where it's beached among epoxy tubes, brushes and X-Acto knives.

Then, cut a plug in the thick glass bubble on the bottom of the float and slide the miniature *Man Who Fell From Heaven* and his cargo of bones inside. Next, fill the float with seawater. Consider spooning sugar into the seawater— sometimes the sea wants sweetness. Norwegian fishermen throw a handful of sugar overboard in a storm. Finally, seal the glass plug into the green globe and set the float right side up. Now, watch the stone man, and the woman in his arms drift forever in a sweet, salted green sea.

Rose raises her knees to ease her back while she considers what to name the glass float construction, and where to place it among the *Women in Glass Vessels*. Some of the pieces are ready. Others are imagined and planned. *Ornament* will be an almost-perfect replica of her mother's last unbroken Vienna glass Christmas decoration, with acrylic gilt standing in for the nineteenth-century mother-of-pearl surface of the first bell, and the tiny twisted glass form of a woman wearing spike-heeled shoes (red plasticine) as the clapper that rings as small, sweet and clear a note as the original. *Crime Scene* is a mirror smeared with Rose's blood, blotted with fingerprints, also hers, and matted with a paper collage of *Vogue* magazine clothes, mostly black, set under cloudy glass in a faux gold baroque frame. *Refugee* is a papier-mâché mermaid who arrived in Prince Rupert last week, postage due, from a Florentine museum reproductions catalogue, and who now wears a face emery-boarded into despair while she lies in a small sand box behind brass-bound, still salt-grimed porthole glass. *Through a Glass* will probably be two ordinary wood-framed kitchen windows, back to back, with blue-and-white checkered curtains. One window may contain Rose's cibachrome print of her mother cleaning the sink, teeth clenched so hard her jaw bulges. Black paper behind the other kitchen window could make dark glass. *Six of One, Half a Dozen of the Other* consists of six bells formed from still faintly scented perfume bottles labelled Joy, Poison, Poeme, Opium, Mitsouko and Vent Vert; six more made out of wide-mouth canning jars. *Damage* is a wide angle black-and-white photograph of a tire iron-smashed windshield, to be displayed horizontally under a ragged-edged print of a woman's face, so overexposed Rose hardly recognized herself even before she heaped hills of glass crushed fine as powdered sugar onto her eyes.

What recorded sound should accompany her and *The Man Who Fell From Heaven*, the two of them lost in the sea green world? A tape already includes samples of stone-shattered windows mixed with glass wind chimes, and a bullet—only a .22—fired through glass, faded under the notes of Rose's mother's crystal glasses singing from the pressure of a wine-soaked finger circling their translucent yellow rims.

And what text for the green glass float full of the sea? So far, all that rises for Rose is, "And before the throne there was a sea of glass like unto crystal..." Revelation 4, 6.

Currents of memory, more than sea or wind, have caught her now:

O western wind, when wilt thou blow
That the small rain down can rain?

Christ, that my love were in my arms
And I in my bed again!

Rose has mumbled this poem aloud on deck on a hundred winter fishing days. She's certain it was made by a man for other men, set down by a sixteenth-century Anonymous, but probably formed much earlier. Muttered first, maybe, by a man standing watch on Hadrian's Wall in a snow-sodden cloak. Or sung by a Hebridean herring fisherman. She wonders if this wind and rain poem has stayed in the minds of the crew dragging perch in Whaleback Deep, north of the fifty-fourth parallel, or the captain who screamed, "You Dog fuckers! Fuck yourselves over the side!" when they slid and fell on the icy decks. But it's more likely draggers and other fishermen might remember, if they remember anything at all about her, that she also knew poems composed by loggers:

(Logging in the rain) "*Pitter, patter, let's get at 'er.*"
(The boss) "*We're here to log, not fuck the dog.*"
(Quitting) "*Slack the main. Call the plane.*"
(Drinking a beer to Greenpeace) "*Big or small, we log 'em all.*"

She received these morsels from the mouth of John Bruce, Richard's father, whose face bones might as well have been hatchet-hacked out of western red cedar, whose favourite photograph of himself, startlingly sharp, black and white and young, showed him standing on a circle of wood not much more than two caulk boots wide, on top of a three hundred-foot cedar spar tree, drinking a beer and laughing. Cedar tree memories go with rain.

It's just another rainy evening
In Cedar, B.C.
I ain't even heard a storm warning yet on the weather tv.
I'm sitting here watching my old canoe
Filling up with rain
Cedar rain
You know it's cold outside
And the fog is blowing down the bay
I don't think I'm gonna make it
Out of here today
   Chorus

This is Ken Hamm's "Rain Blues." Rose forgets how his song ends now. She only remembers, "It's raining, it's pouring, the old man is snoring. Bumped his head and went to bed and couldn't get up in the morning." Rose still misses him. The old man. Richard's father.

Winter fishing evoked no words from John Bruce. Shut inside the slash line of his mouth, even after no matter how many beers in the Harbour Inn, were dark water hills in Queen Charlotte Sound and Hecate Strait with no piece of land or other vessel in sight. Locked up inside, as well, was the litany of the winter marine weather report reciting itself on the radio—CMB, Continuous Marine Broadcasts (a.k.a. CFB, Continued Fucking Bad)—on Coast Guard Radio frequencies.

The Atmospheric Environment Service of Environment Canada provides a pamphlet as a means of translation for Marine Weather broadcasts:

The winds in the marine forecast are the average winds that are expected over the open water. Gusts or squalls are only mentioned when they are expected to be much higher than the average winds. It should be noted that with the rugged coastline of B.C., considerable local variations from the forecast winds are possible....

Light winds—0-11 knots; moderate winds—12-19 knots; strong winds—20-33 knots; gale force winds—34-47 knots; storm force winds—48-63 knots; hurricane force winds—64 knots or more.

But Rose learned for herself soon enough that paper sentences, or words extracted one by one from John Bruce or his son, don't explain winter seas up the coast. She needed to know in her own body the long fall the bow makes down water mountains, and the hoped-for climb that comes next. For literal translation of the marine forecast, she required the hull's punch pounding through her body into her—her of the wind, sea and tide together—and the deep roll that makes her—her of the boat—into a slanted vessel-woman who hesitates with her deck rail down near the sea, then slowly performs the forever-relied-on, "Oh God, she'll come back!" return to upright for an instant before she slants over on her other side.

Lying on the rocks, wrapped in a wind she figures is not

much more than moderate southeast, Rose remembers how at first, Richard was as satisfactorily hard-bitten as his father. "It's raining," Rose announced once when she first came up the coast with him, and he called her from the breakwater pay phone in Alert Bay to walk down to the boat.

"Think you're made of sugar?" Richard asked her. "Think you'll melt?"

No, Rose won't melt, not in the rain anyway. "Rain, rain go away. Come again another day, Little Red Rosie wants to play."

No, she doesn't. She wants to be a changed woman now, not someone who needs to live at no fixed address to avoid disappointing people. She wants fourteen years to have been long enough to learn more than how to escape and keep moving, slipping through the hands of strangers. Or how to stay and be cast into stone. Long enough to choose.

Rose doesn't know yet why she needed the hard coast on this side of the world now, after Mesopotamia and a cargo ship that allowed her to skim the Black and Baltic and other seas with no claim on her. She only knows, has always known since she first set foot on Roberson Point when she was a girl just beginning with Richard, that the full-length stone body in which she lies, *The One Who Fell From Heaven*, is a woman.

Bathed in the black-pearled winter light of early afternoon, the curves cut into the schist, the tilted questioning head, the smallness of the upturned hands and the flung-apart feet all say, "I am a woman."

Pray for her. She fell from heaven, or grace, to complete the contracted price for the secret, unmoving power of stone. Her long hair streamed through the dark, tangling with shattered stars as she fell through heaven's high, green meadows, past arrowed compass points and children who looked up at her from the highest reach of their swings, then returned to their play. She fell slowly, turning in the air, reaching out to touch dyed-to-match satin pumps, gold-strapped sandals and freshly washed runners falling end over end along with her past the jukebox and the band. Languidly and for a long time, she swam through the air, lifting her limbs heavily, as if she were pushing her body through the earth, not the atmosphere, then gradually slowing herself into stone. Now she needs to spill seawater and coins from the hollows of her eyes. The One Who Fell From Heaven *wants to weep her own tears, and be born again into living, moving water, even knowing drowning is one possibility. Pray for her.*

When Rose was a child, moving water meant that there might be more than the present rigid moment. Land stayed steadily the same in one place, and you had to fit into it. But water moved and changed, formed around you, took you into itself and away. Tin Can Creek and the Fraser River and Vancouver Harbour called their intractable selves to her attention from the dissolving borders of the known, solid world. No one at home spoke of them, so they became secret and all the more her own.

The only prayer Rose knows is: On earth as it may be in heaven, moving water changes everything it finds.

The Nighttime Husband

*L*ittle that belongs to the land returns unchanged from the sea. But Rose has heard the story about the time the sea restored, more or less intact, what it had taken from Richard's father, John Bruce.

Johnny had gone down to his boat about midnight, maybe later. The boat was probably one of the wooden seiners called after a cape. Cape Disappointment, Cape St. Elias, Cape Chacon, Cape James, Cape Flattery, Cape Lazo, Cape Scott, Cape Cook, Cape Caution or one of a hundred or more other west coast capes, though not all capes lent their names to boats, and not all cape boats tied at the old breakwater in Alert Bay.

John Bruce was a good fisherman, a captain who had no trouble summoning five or six crewmen to go seining with him every fishing season. He was drunk, too, that night, Richard said, and used to it, so most likely he walked carefully on the tilting floats at the old breakwater. Probably he used all the memory and skill he could muster to navigate the decks, hatch covers and rails of six or seven seiners tied alongside each other to get to his own boat on the outside. Almost certainly, he would have been glad to see his galley where the ridged wooden table was clean, and the bacon was already set out on the counter by the sink, waiting for breakfast before the first set at Fine Beach in the morning. The old oil stove was polished and the galley was warm in the cooling night. This must have happened in late September, almost October, Nimpkish River dog salmon time in Johnstone Strait.

When John lay down in his bunk off the wheelhouse, he might have been thinking his boat was tied to the fishermen's dock at the foot of Main Street this side of Ballantyne Pier in Vancouver. Or he could have believed he was in some narrow-bedded hotel on Hastings East or the bridge end of Granville Street, where by morning you forget the night before. He put his wallet inside his pillow case anyway, although it was safe enough in his pocket while he was lying in his own bunk on his own boat tied at the breakwater down the road from his own house.

He must have forgotten the cigarette he was smoking when he lay down. It had burned its way deep into his pillow by the time his not-so-drunk deckhands rolled onto the boat to smell the stink of charred feathers and find the wheelhouse full of smoke.

They opened the porthole to chuck his pillow overboard then left it open to get some air in there and let him sleep.

At dawn, with the engine fired up, the coffee on, and the deckhands standing by the lines, with John Bruce slowly making his way into the day, the discovery was made. No pillow. No wallet. But wait....

"Look! She's comin' in on the tide!" someone shouts and the pillow, burned, sodden and almost sinking, is pike-poled out of the water with John Bruce's soaked wallet still inside.

There have been other lucky currents and tides. On May 27, 1990, the freighter *Hansa Carrier*, outbound from Korea to Seattle, Washington, lost twenty-one containers overboard in a severe mid-Pacific storm. Thousands of only slightly salt-stained Nike runners, all sizes, rode the Subarctic, Alaska and California currents about two hundred days to shore in Oregon and Washington, and on the west coast of Vancouver Island and the Queen Charlottes. Beachcombers had to search for matching pairs. None of the shoes were tied together. A few runners later reached the northern end of the Big Island of Hawaii.

And in March 1987, near Skidegate Inlet on the west coast of Haida Gwaii, the Queen Charlotte Islands, the Fisheries patrol boat *Sooke Post* put a line on a small open boat last seen a year earlier in Owase, Japan, and still dancing on a four-metre swell. But the long-travelling little wooden boat named *Kazu Maru* can't be said to have come out of the Pacific unchanged. One of her small compartments still contained a fish, but the body of Kazukio Sakamoto, the retired civil servant who loved collecting living specimens of tiny, brightly coloured marine creatures for his saltwater aquarium, was never found.

The captain of the *Sooke Post*, caught in another sorrow, walked to the foot of his neighbour's steps in Queen Charlotte City a year or two later, and shot himself.

The *Kazu Maru* rests in the Mariners' Park above Prince Rupert Harbour now, near the memorial wall. The *Westcoast Fisherman*'s advertisement for the wall reads:

Individual bricks dedicated to those lost at sea can be purchased for $50 each. (Provides for 3 rows of lettering ie. Name: JOHN DOE, Vessel: FISHFINDER, Date of loss: MARCH 1, 1955).

Those lost at sea can be changed beyond recognition in just a day and a night if the sea grinds their flesh over beach sand and rock. Bruising probably can occur even after death when blood flows passively from blood vessels broken against the cliff, or the reef, or the sinking hull. Untended corpses show livor mortis, marine blue blotches where blood pools in the dependent regions of the body, below the heart. Yet a body floating in deep water for days may not reveal much more than "immersion changes," the autopsy pathologist's term for the same wrinkled and swollen skin that appears after a long bath. There are no hungry gulls and crabs in the bath tub though.

Ways to find a body in the river:

Set off dynamite on the bank; the corpse will come to the surface. Float a loaf of bread on the water, then watch where it turns three times. Take a rooster into the search boat, and wait until he crows over the body.

Water can transmute flesh. The soft tissues of an unconsumed body lost long enough in water may chemically change into a hard-surfaced substance called *adipocere,* from the Latin roots for "fat" and "wax." It's possible to find a long-immersed body whose head and internal organs are missing, but with soap-like body fat still clinging to the bones in ceriferous memory of living flesh.

"The sea will give up all its dead one day," wrote St. John the Divine, scratching away at Revelation, 20 in his cave a morning's walk from the Mediterranean in Rome's penal colony on the island of Patmos. This promise, in one form or another, Rose believes.

On the day the ocean surrenders its dead, every old lost pirate, smiling around the knife still between his teeth, will return, along with the boys who fell, or were wind- or sea-swept, from the decks of Canadian corvettes on the North Atlantic run, whose bodies were never recovered and whose families were told they had died in action. The sea will also give up those who were dumped, alive, from Argentinian military planes into the south Atlantic.

It will turn up the sailor who must have been blown off his Greek freighter when it entered Juan de Fuca Strait on a Pacific storm, because he was gone when the river tugs set the ship into a berth at the Fraser-Surrey docks. The B.C. fishermen who stepped out on deck at night to piss, and have never been seen again, drowned or alive, will come back from the sea, too.

"Easiest way to chop a guy on the coast with no questions

asked, even if they find the body," John Bruce once told Rose. "Unzip his jeans and shove."

Rose stowed this information far back in her mind and has never used it, except to ask herself, from time to time, why she keeps it. Departure needs no encouragement. It holds the certainty of sea change, but only the possibility of a comeback. Salt blood, too, can be a means of returning to life.

I've Opened My Veins

I've opened my veins; unstoppably,
Irrestorably, life spurts in sheets.
Bring your basins, bring your plates.
Every plate will be too small.
Every basin too shallow.
    Over the brim—past it—
To the black earth, to nourish the reeds.
Irrevocably, unstoppably,
Irrestorably, verse spurts in sheets.
   — Marina Tsvetayeva

Right now, lying in the petroglyph body on Roberson Point, where even the rain more like misty spray has stopped, Rose can feel a small warm river pouring out of her, pausing, and flowing again. The first day or two of a long offshore swell draws your period, a phenomenon known to Rose and other women who worked on offshore fishing ships. Maybe lying next to the almost incoming tide does the same thing. Salt calling salt.

Rose excavates her clothes for Kleenex, meditating on pockets as identifying characteristics. Like most women who spend time outside of towns and villages up the coast, Rose can dig a tissue out of at least two pockets. Men have to use leaves, or slash the pockets out of their jeans in the bush. Besides the size, missing pockets are how to tell his jeans from hers in the laundry. Men never carry Kleenex, although they usually have a knife with a decent blade in some pocket, along with a forgotten .22 shell and the ring they don't wear on the boat because it can catch on a moving line and tear out a finger.

In Marina Tsvetayeva's pocket, on August 31, 1941, when she was found in a shed in Yelabuga, Russia, hanging from a beam so low she would have needed to bend her knees to slip the noose around her neck, was a blue Morocco leather notebook, 1 x 2 cm, with a minute pencil attached.

Rose croons, "Marina, O Marina...."

I thank you, Lord,
For the Land and the Ocean.
For flesh adored,
For the soul's duration,

Hot blood, cold water,
All of these, together.
I thank you for love.
I thank you for the weather.
    — Marina Tsvetayeva

And thank you for allowing Rose Bachmann, former Canadian Fisheries observer, to learn the comfort of revising history from the Russian stern trawler *Provideniia*'s chief mate, who gave her the tale of Marina Tsvetayeva.

"Zhil-buil," the Russians, including the chief mate's grandmother, say, meaning, "Once upon a time there lived." "Zhil-buil Marina Tsvetayeva," then, whose last landlady, Anastasia Bredelshikova, cannot have spoken the truth about the events in Yelabuga in 1941. Her testimony concerning the nail in the log wall should not be considered reliable, nor her words describing the rope and Marina's bent-kneed stance, nor the unmarked grave in Yelabuga Cemetery.

The truth about Marina Tsvetayeva will be said openly soon, now that the past is moving into the light. The chief mate's grandmother knew all along that Marina lived, smiling a dusty, secret smile from time to time, years after the false record of her death in Yelabuga. Similar cases were common in those years. Many were lost who did not yet lie safe in the ground. But Marina Tsvetayeva could not have hanged herself on August 31, 1941. She still had semolina, sugar and rice, as Bredelshikova reported, and half a panful of cooked fish. She had poetry.

The years beyond 1941 are sketchy, to be sure. There are unanswered questions. Why was she sentenced to the Magadan prison camp in Siberia? Still, that scarcely matters now. She wasn't short of company there, some as well known as herself, others near to nameless. What caused Marina to crack her silence one day (1950?), and say the words that gathered the other prisoners, silent themselves for years by then, to listen to her? We will not likely learn why Marina's poems rose "irrevocably, unstoppably" again on that day in the camp, neither must we grieve that the Magadan poems are lost. They belonged only to the women who were with her then.

The reports connecting Tsvetayeva to the Amur River settlements must be dismissed. It's improbable that a woman her age would have had the strength to walk so far. Besides, the Amur River tales date from the time she was almost certainly employed in some capacity at a fish plant on the Kamchatka coast. Restriction of movement was usual for those released from camps in the area.

The Kamchatka references explain Marina's contact with the Chukchi people of Siberia, and what they call her "true death," although they won't produce a body as proof. She flew away, the Chukchi say, after their Old Woman sang the spell that relieved her of the relentless need to live in order to make poems. Marina Tsvetayeva's bird soul pecked an opening in the translucent membrane between this world and the other, the Chukchi tell, and she left us.

Doing up her jeans, Rose is still chanting a Marina litany, "Aphrodite Marina, Mari the Sea, Mother Mariamne, Marah, Mariham, Mary, Miriam, Mari Goddess, Maria Sea, Stella Maris." Arms around her knees, she sits on the beach beside the petroglyph who is *The Woman Who Fell From Heaven*. Once upon a time, another woman sat like this on the beach at Metlakatla, watching the entrance to Prince Rupert Harbour.

Long ago a Tsimshian princess sat alone on the beach in front of her village. Behind her, were cedar longhouses and children laughing as they ran around the cooking fires. In front of her were the changing waters of the northern sea. Her house was set apart from the others because she was considered special by all of her people. Even so, she was lonely. The time had come for her to marry and have children of her own, but there seemed to be no man right for her. Young noblemen came from villages as far away as Alaska to ask if she would marry them, but the young woman was wise as well as beautiful. She listened to her grandmother, who said, "Feel their hands! A smooth-handed man is soft and weak and will never make a good husband for you." So when the young men came to her, stepping proudly from their canoes loaded with gifts of sea otter pelts and abalone shells, the princess felt their hands. All the young men were too wellborn to work. Their hands were smooth, so she would have none of them. She sat on the beach alone and looked at the sea.

She sat on the beach looking at the sea, clearly recalling that she was never a wise or beautiful young woman. Later, a long time without mirrors on the north Pacific Ocean, and a man she met years after she was young, would make her beautiful, sometimes, in a certain light, but even now, any embankments of wisdom Rose maintains around herself are quite likely to be breached by a flood of impulse.

There were no grandmothers for Rose. A long time ago, pages of soft paper covered with spiked black words had been mailed from places so small they had no names, Rose's mother said. Once, there was a handkerchief—stiff, yellowed linen embroidered with pink rosebuds, their satin-stitch plumpness flattened in the overseas journey, but the french-knotted thorns on the stems still perfect. With the handkerchief came advice, translated by her father:

Meine liebe kleine Enkelin! Mache deiner satinstiche ruhig... Dearest small Granddaughter! Make your satin stitches so evenly and calmly, one tight to another. For french knots: twist the thread three times around the needle; hold the bundle of threads with the edge of your thumb, pushing lightly and slowly until it slides off the needle through linen stretched in an ivory embroidery hoop. Pull firm. With love.

At nineteen, Rose embroidered strawberries with seductive french-knot dimples onto the cuffs of antique velvet dresses. The flattened silk pile of the black or burgundy velvet—or Rose's favourite dark green—no longer responded to steaming, and did nothing to disguise her brittle thinness. Her red-brown hair hung down her back in tangled rattails, pinned up haphazardly with trembling hands before she went to the house on Arbutus Street for Sunday dinner.

On Sundays, Rose's mother said, "It would look so much smarter if you got it cut," and "Remind me to give you one of those white pencils for under your nails," and "What are your plans?" She meant, Rose understood, "What are you going to do about your hair, your fingernails, and about making it up to us?" Rose knew she was responsible for disappointments requiring compensation: not being a boy; being the only child; and not living up to a name that seemed to hope for tightly furled, delicately coloured petals. These complaints in themselves were unsatisfactory: no police, no pregnancy, nothing dramatic enough to arouse the shocked, pleasurable sympathy of others. Rose never answered her mother's questions.

"What are your hobbies?" her father sometimes asked, as if she were a new, unaccounted for acquaintance, or a client whose tangled taxes necessitated the provision of a slight, formal distraction. As if she were not the same daughter who used to listen to his story about the choosing of her name. As if she hadn't tried to believe she could turn herself into Rosa, a girl he glimpsed one afternoon on the other side of the war, turning cartwheels in a stone square, tumbling the flame-coloured petals of her skirt over her head for the boy watching her, holding out a dusty hand for coins when she was done. The last words of the name story were always, "But that was in another country, Rosa, Röschen, Röslein."

That Rosa would have had pinky red petals and butter-cream knees and thighs, Rose imagined when she was ten, hiding in the carport, waiting for her mother to stop being angry and come out to drive her to the library. She watched her father walk down the glossy grey back steps and enter the chicken-wire circle enclosing his roses on a shaven lawn. He knelt in the black loam hills around the bushes to lean into jagged-edged leaves and full-blown flowers never allowed into the house unless they were taken as buds. He was breathing them all into himself, Rose thought, or perhaps he was only fingering the balsa wood tags, each one bearing a name in sharp slanted black script: *Complicata, Rosa Mundi, Rose du Roi, Fantin-Latour, Maiden's Blush.*

On Sundays, Rose's knife and fork clattered too loudly on reproduction Meissen plates. Her mouth dried and her throat constricted around spaetzle and stale hazelnut torte. She swallowed doughy lumps while she practised forgiving her father for forgetting the start of the naming story. The beginning was always his promise that she would be his wild Canadian Rosa because she was a bud born in the new world the year the Russians and the others left Vienna. Perhaps he hadn't forgotten the promise, only changed its terms to accord with his disenchantment when his rosebud child lengthened, sprouted and began to live up to a name that had likely belonged to a dirty gypsy, her mother said, and should be changed to plain Rose.

Rose on the beach at Roberson Point thinks she should have answered her father, "Guilt and daydreams and escape plans are my hobbies."

On Arbutus Street Sundays, Rose's hipbones, knees and elbows sharpened into defensive angles. Her shoulders hunched under the weight of her lies. It was a lie that a haircut was on the horizon; that she was perfectly happy living in an English Bay apartment downtown with three other girls; that she was learning data processing at business college, not art history, colour theory and graphic design part-time at Emily Carr Art & Design school. It was a lie, too, that Rose never noticed her mother's silent anger thickening and solidifying when her husband left his office earlier and earlier to sleep away even weekday afternoons.

And another Sunday lie that she had not noticed *Fantin-Latour* and *Rosa Mundi* and the others dry and untended in the chicken-wire sanctuary garden.

It was true that nineteen-year-old Rose was softer, less barricaded territory on other nights of the week, in other parts of the city. Her body's angles eased under imitation Tiffany lamps in damp basement suites, or on the floors of attic rooms in Fourth Avenue communal houses where cushions and futons were covered with wax-spattered Indian print cotton, or in cement-floored warehouses where carefully torn Janis Joplin posters and strangers' faces were intermittently lit by stolen, slow spinning disco lights. In these night places, Rose walked on clouds of reefer, roofers, doobies, ganja, Northern Lights, Skunk, puff, smoke, hash, hashish, New Style, seedless, Mexican drag, mary jane, marijuanna, mary d'ya'wanna? Rosie d'ya wanna? and drifted at ease on tides of red wine and Joni Mitchell songs. Night was safer than day, she thought then.

At night, she was in the habit of whispering, "I love you" if the engineering student or the guitar player or the guy who knew all the words to "Dark of the Moon" said it first, and if the tips of her breasts were already hard in his hands. She thought, then, that her own body's flickering and opening in response to the nearness of another, combined with the word love, could be translated into a getaway. She had a weakness for unshaven men in shirt sleeves who crashed the party, or wandered into the wrong club, saying to her, "Do you know how drunk you are when I'm good-looking?" or "Starkle, starkle little twink. Who the hell you are, I think," before they stumbled out. They were soldiers returning to another front, she decided some nights when she was awash in dream smoke, and she could catch up to them and never miss the crowded rooms she had left behind. Sparkling, she would be, in the night, running ahead of those men, then allowing herself to be caught and held for a while, to be another Rose.

It was also true that holding moving water still with a Pentax Spotmatic from Pacific Pawn on Main was easier than becoming another Rose. She stood over the Fraser River on the Pattullo Bridge in New Westminster, the Knight Street Bridge in Vancouver, the river bank at Annieville and the Fraser-Surrey docks, stopping the water flow with her camera. She turned the river current white, then silver and finally flat black in the Emily Carr darkroom. She halted the tide from the top of the lighthouse under Lions Gate Bridge, and stilled waves into static matte finish mounds off Point Atkinson. She was considering long exposures and grainy archival paper to turn Vancouver Harbour to sand dunes on the Saturday when she found Richard.

Richard was not a man too wellborn to work, and his hands, even half the length of the dock ladder away from Rose, looked warm and strong. Neither the hands, nor the dark hair nor the stocky arms loading net web onto a wooden boat deck at Campbell Avenue fish dock were ever recognizable as more than blurred motion in the photographs Rose took of him that day. The heavy-boned blank face and shuttered eyes looking up at her, then away, after the first long camera click, never appeared in the pictures. For a moment, Rose thought he was someone she almost remembered or had always needed without knowing it...Pierre-Esprit Radisson, maybe, back from months in the dark woods around Fort Bourbon on the Nelson River in the winter of 1670/71, or Sonny Liston before the Miami Beach fight.

"I'm sorry," she said to the man on the boat, her first lie to him. He turned away from her and kept on working. The dismissal drew Rose another step down the ladder. Her hair, the camera strap and her sleeves jagged on the rusty, barnacled rung she clutched.

"Coffee?" he asked, and reached for her hand to haul her over the deck rail. A long time afterward, Rose would come to understand this invitation as an act of courage and almost courtly civility from a man astonished by the presence of a scrawny girl in a velvet dress photographing strangers on the waterfront.

That night, the Metlakatla princess covered herself with her fur robe and fell asleep to dream of a husband whose face she couldn't see. Perhaps she thought she was still dreaming when someone lay down beside her. She felt his warm, rough-skinned hands on her body, so she knew this man was meant to be her husband.

Richard came to Rose that same night on the boat. He knelt on the slatted deck beside the bunk to cradle her with one arm under her shoulders and the other in the crook of her knees. He rocked her sharp bones and tightly clenched flesh in time with the small, repeated motions of the boat moving in the harbour wake until the set of her mouth softened, until her thighs slacked and the openings of her body loosened. If Rose expected, then, a tongue to touch and slowly enter her mouth, if she thought fingers would pet her breasts, then paddle in the damp place between her legs, what she got was a warm weight almost enclosing her beneath him, then pushing himself into her.

Richard kept his face hidden when he finished. Rose didn't care. The retreat, return motion of the keel beneath her and the certainty of undersea the other side of the hull next to her body interested her more. Richard whispered some words she couldn't hear before he rolled out of the bunk. He covered her with a slightly damp, diesel-smelling sleeping bag. Rose laid her cheek against the cold bulkhead to hear the hull creak against the pier, and slept.

The engines shuddered and screamed. Rose sat up so fast she slammed her head on the bunk above her. Richard was a dark figure in the doorway, outlined by the engine room light. "...tide," he was shouting. "Do you want to get off?" Rose shook her head. She stepped off the boat a few minutes later, but only onto the Coal Harbour fuel barge to find the pay phone and turn her back on the awakening city.

Her father would still be asleep in ironed pyjamas, she knew, but her mother's voice was already hard and bright. "I won't be there for supper tonight, Mama," Rose said. "I'm going away for a while. Just up the coast." She added, "I have a ride," as if this were information her mother would value.

"What are you talking about?"

"Maybe I'll get a job up there."

"Maybe? Nothing is organized. The way you are. Always." Her mother's contempt bit and spat the words into Rose's ear. "Where kind of place are you going to? Where will you stay?"

On an boat, an ark holding a whole world to carry Rose away.

"Is this some kind of romance idea?" her mother asked. "What are your plans?"

"I'll write," Rose said, and hung up.

There were no plans. There was only Lions Gate Bridge with Richard's white *Florentina* and a Japanese container ship outbound beneath it. There was the lighthouse on the Stanley Park side where Rose had climbed to photograph the tide into stillness, and the same water moving now, bearing away the boats, the freighter crew and Richard and Rose. There was the harbour spilling itself into wider, white-capped water, and Rose ferrying coffee from the galley along the deck to Richard in the wheelhouse. The *Florentina* slammed herself along. Rose stumbled on the sill of the wheelhouse door and the coffee she'd already drunk tilted and rolled in her belly.

"Georgia Strait," Richard announced, taking the cup from her hand and gently pushing her toward the window ledge where she could hold on. He pulled the window halfway down and jammed a knife in the wooden frame to hold it open. "Breathe," he ordered. "Look at the horizon line, not the salt chuck or the boat."

Rose gulped cool damp air and made herself remember that the Spanish explorers called these waters after a woman. The strait named Gran Canal de Nuestro Senora del Rosario la Marinera, for the Virgin of the Sailors' Rosary only became Georgia later, courtesy of Captain George Vancouver. She kept this historical comfort, and the fact that she was feeling better, almost normal, to herself. Richard couldn't be allowed to learn the ways in which she managed, even if this morning he was satisfactorily a pirate keeping his eyes on the sea, not her, even if he wore a black denim jacket with an upturned collar, and even if he had combined tenderness, rough handling and silence in the bunk last night. Rose was probably safe now, established as the cherished, only explorer who could cut a track into Richard's wilderness. She quivered her lower lip, to appear as if she might be afraid of choppy water, or the green smudge of islands too far away to swim for in cold water, or of him, and not of being sent back to be Rose Bachmann telling lies in the city.

"What'll happen now?" she asked in a voice she made small.

"We might not make the tide in the narrows," Richard said. "Have to get through after dark."

We could try, Rose thought, believing that a fourteen-knot tide could be negotiated with, or tricked into ignoring the vessels caught in it.

"We'll be in the Bay around midnight."

The Bay at Granville and Georgia in Vancouver still sells Balmain's Vent Vert, the wild green rising scent of green wind, new wind, Garcia Lorca's *Somnambulist Ballad* green.

The Bay on Jasper Avenue in Edmonton gave Rose a student job last summer, once she explained about the long bus ride and said that she'd told her parents she had the job already. Most of the money from stocking shelves at the Bay went for a room at the YWCA and summer dresses to be happy in during white hot Alberta days and summer lightning nights.

"Alert Bay," Richard said. He leaned ove to put his arm around her. "It'll be all right," he murmured into the nest of tangles at the back of her neck. Rose let herself lean into him. His heart thumped into her head in time with the beat of the engine under her feet. His jacket smelled like diesel and cigarettes and spilled beer. He wouldn't know all the words to "Raised on Robbery" or any other Joni Mitchell song. He wouldn't go out to the garden wearing a cuff-linked shirt and a fixed, patient smile to tend old-fashioned roses. But Rose would not be a disappointment to him. She would always be an unexpected miracle, never a known quantity. And part of him, the farthest dark reach of his wilderness, would remain suitably unavailable to her. She didn't need to tell him, "I love you," to accelerate emotion.

"I love you, Rose," Richard whispered when the lights in Alert Bay broke into the night.

All night he stayed with her, but in the hour before dawn he left saying, "You must never see my face or I shall not be able to come to you again." When the sun was up, the princess came out of her little house to find an enormous halibut lying on the beach in front of her door. She smiled to see the present from her night-time husband and ran to tell her grandmother about the man who had come to her in the night. Soon all the Tsimshians knew. Their curiosity was great and the princess told of her husband's warning never to look on his face. She shared the halibut with everyone in the village and that night her husband came again and left before morning light. This time she found a pile of spring salmon in front of her door.

Every night he came. Every morning there was a gift from the sea for the princess. She and her grandmother traded the fish for all they needed, and became wealthy. The young woman was happy, but her grandmother never ceased to wonder about the nighttime husband. She gave her granddaughter a small stone pot filled with red ochre to mark the nighttime husband so they might know him in the daylight. The princess put a dab of red paint on the back of her husband's head and the next day her grandmother looked carefully at all the young men in the village, but none was marked with red paint. Messengers travelled to other villages further north and along the great rivers, but they found no man with the red sign. At last the grandmother could live with her curiosity no longer. She crept from the longhouse to hide herself behind a tree on the beach when the stars were still shining on Metlakatla Pass. As always, the nighttime husband left his wife asleep in her furs and stepped out of their little house alone, but the grandmother couldn't see him clearly in the dark. When the thin light of dawn opened the sky, she heard a splash as someone entered the sea. The next night again she looked out from her hiding place. This time she saw him. The nighttime husband was the sea bear—the grizzly with a fin on his back.

He was towing a whale for the princess's morning gift. The great bear saw the grandmother watching him. He roared with anger and sorrow, loud enough to shake the tall cedars. For the last time, he stood on the beach, and the waking villagers listened, trembling, to his roaring song of farewell to his wife. He returned to the sea, where his body became rock which the Tsimshians ever after called Bear Rock.

Bear Rock is still here, charted now as Barrett Rock in the harbour entrance around the corner from Rose in Venn Pass.

The qualities of husbands, not wives, are the first focus in the Tsimshian nighttime husband story; in the Cupid and Psyche legend that bears some of the same erotic and emotional freight, and in the story Rose told herself while she was still married to Richard. The sea bear husband was warm in the night, gone by morning, and generous with the rich food he provided. Psyche's "destined husband...came only in hours of darkness and fled before the dawn of morning, but his accents were full of love, and inspired a like passion in her." Cupid told his wife, "If you saw me, perhaps you would fear me, perhaps adore me, but all I ask of you is to love me."

Love was approximately all Richard asked of Rose. He provided her with warmth in the night. He brought home fish and deer meat, as well as money for food, and Debbie Harry with Blondie's "Heart of Glass" and a hundred other songs. In salmon summers and herring winters, he satisfied his wife's wish for a hard-faced man who asked her almost no questions, and gave her his absence.

What Is True Up the Coast

Rose waited for him by the phone, or watched the harbour from apartments in Alert Bay and Prince Rupert when Johnstone and Hecate Straits were rippled salt lakes and the other seiners had already come in, and when the water was torn black silk and none of the boats were home yet. The windows in these rooms were bare on the water side, allowing the sea and the paler sky and wind to enter, washing light and blown rain over the brown betty tea pot, over books, jars of pencils and Rose in an embroidered linen nightgown, sitting with her knees to her chest in a round-backed wooden captain's chair. The chair had gone grey and rough in the rain at the abandoned logging camp in Beware Pass where Richard had found it, and lashed it down on the back deck to bring into the Bay. Little else of him was left behind in his home when he was gone.

Through ten years of salmon and herring seasons, she waited and watched to find out whether the *Florentina* had crossed over from Masset Inlet, or gone south to the sockeye opening at Nitinat, or north to Rivers Inlet and Hakai Pass. Rose received word sometimes from radio messages sent to other fishing widows. The widows met her on the waterfront road in Alert Bay, or on the wooden steps down to Cow Bay in Prince Rupert, offering, "Full moon and empty arms," or, "Home tonight." Fishing fleet news surfaced at B.C. Packers, (Busy Pluckers, Richard called the fish company, or Beastly Fuckers) or from the Fisheries office where Rose recorded catch and spawning numbers. News of Richard himself, the little he allowed, came in the front door with him.

"How was it?" Rose would ask into a mouthful of silver-scaled wet wool jacket and warm skin.

"Not bad," Richard might say or, "Got a few," or, "Loaded her. Only humps though."

The first year, Rose asked about storms. "Enough wind to keep the flies off the deck," or, "New guy got sick all the way across the Sound. He can't steer for shit anyway," were Richard's responses. In the winters, if Rose wept luxurious tears to see him warm and walking on the land again, he might add, "It's not rough until you're standing on the wheelhouse door." Once, in the kitchen, he turned his back so he could tell her, "Green water over the wheelhouse once or twice," but she didn't know, then, that green water wasn't waves or swells or spray, but undersea.

Richard knew secrets about the wind and the sea, Rose assumed, and the gliding minds of sockeye, spring, coho, humpback and dog salmon and herring. He kept these matters, and any fear or love he felt about them, from her. She let his secrets lie. Pirates and soldiers don't come home to tell the whole truth by the fire. They wouldn't be real pirates and soldiers if they did. She never asked if she faded from him on the boat, dissolved into a blurred memory by that shifting water-coloured other world. Maybe she only became real again when he climbed the steps to the top floor apartment in the old customs house in Alert Bay, or the drafty wind-shaken house on Beach Street in Prince Rupert. He never asked her why the doors to both places had to be painted in yellow, crimson and azure-bordered rectangles and squares from a picture Rose found in *Tales From the Arabian Nights*.

The wordless marriage covenant between these two required a script in which the husband hid at least half of himself offstage in darkness, while the wife, not admitting she had any secrets of her own, performed a monologue in the theatre of feeling on behalf of both of them. Rose, rounder now, her hair and clothes smelling of sandalwood incense, needed reassurance about the lateness of sockeye runs and the nearness of income tax and bank payments. Winter-grey streets, seas and skies, falling fish prices, and the empty, ill-lit field in the far back country of her mind necessitated nightgowns and sheets tie-dyed scarlet and cerise. The dye bloomed in bursts of colour wherever skin touched heated skin, meaning Richard must sponge these warm hidden places with his tongue, transferring red stains to his mouth and cheeks until Rose laughed so hard he had to laugh, too.

The unspoken bargain between them permitted, perhaps demanded, that Richard contradict himself, that he be a man who used his marine radio to tell the fishing fleet north of Cape Caution that he had won Rose playing Indian poker at the SeaGate Hotel in Port Hardy, but who never played cards for money again, not even craps, or liar's poker with the serial numbers on dollar bills, after the day he brought her to Alert Bay. It demanded that he be a husband who took away, somewhere, the pistol and switchblade Rose found wrapped in his bannockburn wool winter fishing pants, then showed his wife how to thread her sewing machine and make a fried egg sandwich:

Get the toast ready while the eggs are in the pan, coming done. Break the yolk. Flip the eggs and let them set, sunny side down, on gentle heat for a moment. Salt and pepper generously. One, or one and a half or two eggs to a sandwich depending on appetite.

Except for baking, Rose's cooking was a scrape-along affair with neccessary time gaps between the (at first, always too dry) venison roast on the table, the meaty, metallic familiar-from-her-own-body smell of blood on butchering day in the kitchen, and the fresh-killed deer hanging from the rigging on the back deck in the dark. The gutted flanks seemed to sigh with breath, still, even when Rose knew only the sway of the boat in tide chop was moving them, even when Richard was yelling, "Get in off that deck, Rose. Or at least let me know when you're goin' out there at night, for Christ's sake."

But baking transformed earthly raw matter and story scraps into a portion of paradise. Angel food cake:

Combine flour, sugar, and one and a half cups of egg whites. (The boat name for eggs is boneless baby chickens). Beat the whites into peaks with two forks held back to back if without an egg beater.

She made walnut or lemon curd or maple squares, layers of pastry pressed into pans, then spread with sweet riches, and topped with coconut meringue or flaked almonds or icing. The icing will be either a delicate, slightly brittle frosting, flavoured with the memory of maiden Anglican missionary women after the Great War, or a sturdy new world invention:

Mix one-quarter of a cup canned milk with one-third of a cup melted butter, two-thirds of a cup brown sugar, half a package flaked coconut and a drop of vanilla Spread over warm cake. Broil five minutes. Watch carefully when the wood stove flares, or the oil stove flickers low, or the boat rolls.

Make Sex in a Pan the way gillnetters do: bake white or yellow cake mix in a big pan, then cover with vanilla pudding, also from a mix, and well-drained crushed pineapple. Top with whipped cream and chill.

Make bread. Give us this day: the bread and gravy called Oakalla Penitentiary pudding; the bread and jam called Kingcome Inlet pie; the bit of bread in children's pockets that protects them from fairy magic, say the Newfoundland trawlermen working out here now. Give us the plastic-wrapped loaf of McGavin's white sliced that Georgie Moran sprayed frozen with the CO2 fire extinguisher on his gillnetter, then chucked onto the deck of the American yacht that hailed him in the middle of Blackfish Sound to ask if he had any bread to spare. Give us the Americans' astonished faces as they ask Georgie, "However is there room for a freezer on that tiny little old boat?" Give us the loaf of black bread a Russian captain, lacking Metaxa brandy or vodka, presented to the Canadian pilot after he guided the grain ship from Prince Rupert Harbour to Triple Island. Restore the value of this bread as it rolls, unregarded, round and heavy as home, off the deck of the pilot boat into the sea.

Grow bread from flour, water, (save the potato water for bread, is Richard's advice) salt and yeast. About the yeast, Richard's mother, Lillian, laughing her head off, says, "Know ye not that a little leaven leaveneth the whole lump?" 1 Corinthians 5,6. "Don't waste two tablespoons of yeast to make four loaves of bread, Rose." Use less and let it rise longer. Use things up. Wear them out. Make them do, or do without.

Richard in those years, a husband of some experience by now, makes do twice over: building a fire with wet wood in the rain on Port Essington beach not long after he and Rose have moved up to Prince Rupert and making bread in a frying pan over that fire. Flour, salt, sugar and baking powder. Warm water and a gentle hand. Poke the dough with a fork. Fry it until done. Call it bannock.

"Who showed you how to do that?" Rose, drying her

hair under a cedar branch hanging down onto the beach some way back from the fire, wonders, without much urgency, if she shouldn't know at least this much about Richard by now.

After four years, he knows she was a bookish city child who saw fires only behind a brass screen in the fireplace. He knows she lied about homework and the Kerrisdale library to ride her bike to Tin Can Creek seeping past Eddy's Nursery into the Fraser. He knows she rode further, on larger lies, to the lookout on Marine Drive, the very place where Simon Fraser stepped from his canoe to see the river opening into the Pacific. He probably doesn't know that she climbed over the guardrail, down the bank, looking for the dangerous brilliance of Fraser's journey to be still shining out of the ground, for the sound of paddle splashes hanging in the air, along with the smokey smell of distance. Rose hoped that standing on the river bank where Simon Fraser had stood might change her into a braver, brighter eleven year old girl. Prettier, too.

Richard doesn't know, because Rose herself doesn't remember, that when she was a child she believed explorers didn't really die on the last page of their biographies. Simon Fraser, Alexander MacKenzie, and David Thompson continued their travels on other rivers somewhere, no matter the cold or the snags or the rapids up ahead. The pushing, insistent idea of a journey kept them going forever, kicked out their cooking fires in the morning, lifted their hands to shadow eyes looking ahead, never back. The explorers, and the voyageurs and coureurs de bois who came after them, would all have seen the possibilities of courage in Rose Bachmann, child explorer. They would have overlooked her clumsiness. Simon and Alec and David would have known that her yearning for anywhere beyond Kerrisdale was an asset, not an oddity, because they were daydreamers too. Deep inland, behind the factor's desk in Hudson Bay and Northwest Company trading posts, in air thick with the beloved stink of furs, smoke and gun oil, or around polished tables in company meeting rooms up stone staircases in Montreal, these men had imagined long, west-falling rivers and the shifting, transformative blue slide of the Pacific Ocean.

But Richard knows useful things, not daydreams. He doesn't ever say how he learned them, or much about his childhood or any time before Rose. He doesn't talk about the brother with fair skin and hair and Richard's own axe-carved features, seen in Lillian's photo album. He hardly mentions Lillian, his still-blonde, still-itinerant mother, who sometimes comes back to Alert Bay from Vancouver to advise Rose.

"Advice from Lillian Before, or Lillian After?" Richard asks Rose when his mother's gone. Lillian Before laughs a lot while she advises Rose on baking, on how to revive not-too-deeply passed out people with an ammonia-soaked rag, and on using Preparation H for the bags under her eyes. It's mostly dogfish oil, after all, and meant to shrink tender tissues. Lillian After quotes Twelve-Step slogans and the Bible, and still laughs.

Richard tells stories about his father. The Time John

Bruce Lost His Wallet and the Tide Brought It Back, The Time John Drummed a Drowning Man Back on Board with the Seine Net, The Time John Fell in Love with Mona Lisa (the Nat King Cole version) Until Lillian Used his Record for Target Practice with her .22.

Rose thinks they've come north to Prince Rupert to get away from these legends. Richard thinks they loaded the *Florentina* with cardboard boxes, the rain-worn captain's chair and duffle bags full of Rose's photographs and paint brushes, to steam north so he can fish the Nass and Skeena, and Rose can get a full-time job.

The cedar branches hanging over the beach at Port Essington are so thick around Rose not much rain comes in. Through the network of green lace, she can see Richard crouched over his fire, slanting the black cast iron pan over low, licking flames. Rain hisses soft into the fire and steams in tiny spurts on the bannock's swelling crust. In a moment, he will bring the fry bread and a Thermos of clam chowder into the cedar shelter. Rose will be fed and warm. Richard will see to it. The tree will enclose both of them.

Rose won't be alone, running on an empty, dark plain, the way she is sometimes in her dreams. Richard will see to this, too. He's never lost in his dreams, only tangled in 240 fathoms of seine net, the way fishermen are in their night-mares. Once, he was under a dream sea where a woman with long, dark, caressing hair and white, white skin wanted him to stay. His pillow was soaked with tears, or salt water, when he woke. But this was before he knew her, he has said to Rose, who never told him about her own night exile.

Richard now crawls into the nest under the branches, carrying the bannock on a bark slab, the Thermos, and a scrap of nineteenth-century lace curtain Rose found on Port Essington's rotting boardwalk before the rain began. He arranges the lace, which he has dried on sticks at the edge of the fire, over Rose's hair, then unbuttons her jeans so he can warm his hands on her belly and at the small of her back. They are both safe from their dreams here, on the beach at Port Essington on the south bank of the Skeena River.

Port Essington is empty except for the two of them. Cunningham's fur trading post and store, two or three salmon canneries, the docks for wood-burning stern-wheelers carrying Omineca gold-seekers and hookers upriver, the hotels, cafés, the Grand Trunk Pacific Railway workers' bar, the Anglican church, and the bay-windowed houses are gone. Their fir and cedar posts, planks and beams have burned, or dissolved into the river or been choked by unceasing green. Richard, Rose and the remnants of Port Essington are surrounded, in late summer, by fern forests and thickets of salal, devil's club, huckleberries, salmonberries, two kinds of blueberries—blue-black and bright blue—carpet and highbush cranberries, cloud berries, and soopolallie berries, as well as the bead lilies called Skeena flowers and rich-smelling skunk cabbage that reminds Rose of Tin Can Creek.

Port Essington, the two rivers place where the Ecstall flows into the Skeena on the other side of the water from the highway, is hard enough to reach to satisfy Richard, and contains enough stories to content Rose. There are women here to keep her company. In its high times, Port Essington has landed opera singers and the occasional painted city woman selling raffle tickets, although there was actually, no raffle. Missionary women, teachers and hundreds of women and girls who worked in the canneries lived in Essington. Even Emily Carr was here, staying overnight with some niece or other whose husband managed a cannery while she waited for the steamer to take her upriver to Hazelton, where she would go on to Kitwancool by wagon.

Rose torments herself wondering if she would have had the courage, and the vision, to fall in love with Emily's work if she'd first seen *Kitwancool, Laughing Forest, Forest Interior in Shafts of Light* and the others when they were new. At the Vancouver art school named for Emily Carr, Rose had usually decided gloomily that she would have likely missed the point. She would have been the scrawny Jerusalem dancing girl who figured Jesus was a trouble-maker, and bad for business, or the fish-and-chip waitress in Victoria who dismissed Emily Carr as a peculiar old woman without much money who wouldn't have cared what Rose thought anyway.

Under the cedar tree on the river beach at Port Essington, Rose has a little more hope for her imaginary past self. Besides, Elizabeth Spalding is here, too. She was born behind Port Essington, at Spokechute, the Tsimshian village called the last river camp and she likes Rose well enough to ask her into her house at Gitsumgalum up near Terrace to listen to stories—her own, and the river's, and others.

About the river, Elizabeth says, "Skeena River was hard sometimes. No store was on the reserve, or at Port Essington in the winter, so you needed to go down the river to Prince Rupert on the coast. We did go in ourselves to get Christmas that time, and another boat went in, but they missed the tide. My husband, he made us leave Rupert just before the tide changed, and we followed it home. That way is safe. There's ice on the river, and if you miss the tide, it can come down and crush the boat. That's what happened to the others. The ice caught the boat. Peter Spalding and his wife; Bennet and his wife, Lucy; Matt Wesley and the others. Nine of them. They found Peter. He jumped off the boat onto the ice, and he froze there, that's why they found him. They never found the others."

Elizabeth Spalding is the one who lets Rose know about the woman in a box:

In the time when the Tsimshian clans were making themselves known, the chief of Gitsumgalum village on the Skeena River, was an old man whose youngest and most beautiful wife was a woman of the Eagle clan. Before she was married, this woman had tamed a young eagle and twisted her own copper bracelet around one of his talons to mark him. The eagle stayed near to her whether she was tending the cooking fires, or picking berries on the mountain or standing alone on the river bank, watching the water. Although the old chief was proud of his wife's beauty, she turned her thoughts to his nephew after her first married winter. When the chief was away, these two met in secret and loved one another. The chief was a great hunter, so when his traps were sprung empty, and his arrows missed the deer, he knew all was not well at home. He returned to the village to announce his plans for a journey to new hunting grounds many days distant. He hid himself in the forest, then crept back into the village that night to discover the lovers together. In his rage, he stabbed his nephew and flung the body into the river, but he couldn't raise his knife against the beautiful Eagle Woman. He put her into a carved cedar storage box, and there was only time for the older women to thrust in some dried berries and a small knife before the box was laced with deerhide thongs and thrown into a canoe. The chief pushed the canoe out into the Skeena's spring flood.

Inside the box, Eagle Woman crouched, trembling, as the canoe rushed downriver. She slept, woke in the dark and slept again until the canoe began to rock slowly from side to side. She wept with fear and felt about the box to find the knife, slashed the binding thongs and raised the box lid. The canoe was rolling on wide saltwater swells and she could see no land. Eagle Woman sank down in the box, covering her face with her hands, until she heard the harsh cry of an eagle above her. She raised her head and took heart, ate a handful of berries and cupped her hands to drink rainwater. Many times the day faded to night and dawned again as the huge bird and the woman crossed the sea together. Eagle Woman was faint with cold and hunger when the waves tossed her canoe onto the sand at Rose Spit on Haida Gwaii, the Queen Charlotte Islands. A Haida chief found the canoe and the cedar box and the weakened young woman with a copper-banded eagle circling above her. "Carry her to the village," he ordered his nephews, *"and let the bird be."*

So a woman of the Eagle clan came to the Haida people and married one of their noblemen while the eagle watched over her days. She bore three children, two boys and a girl, and taught them the language of the Tsimshian as well as the Haida. As the boys grew to manhood, others said to them, "Where are your uncles? Has your mother no brothers?" humiliating Eagle Woman and her children until she went to her Haida husband, saying, "My children must have their own place. We will return to my home."

The Haida man loved his wife well and worked with her to gather much wealth so she could return to the Tsimshian with a high heart. Together, they loaded a huge canoe with sea otter furs, with the Haida hunting clothes made from sea lion skin which no claw or arrow can pierce and with dried halibut and other rich food. Eagle Woman and her three children set out in the canoe, and the copper-banded eagle guided their journey across the sea to the place where the Skeena empties into saltwater. They rested one night beside the river at Spokechute. The next day, they paddled upstream to Gitsumgalum village, where the Tsimshian people stood on the riverbank, watching the Haida canoe approach. Eagle Woman sang the song of her family, and the Tsimshian knew her again, and were pleased with her gifts. In this way, Eagle Woman returned to Gitsumgalum with her children. Yet her travels were not over. She lived a while with the people on the Nass River, and bore children of the Eagle clan there. Later, she was captured by the Kitimaat and had other Eagle children with them. She came again to Gitsumgalum when she was old, where the eagle wearing her copper bracelet *watched over her until she died.*

Richard let Rose tell him the tale of the woman in a box and the eagle and the river, and a hundred other true stories he'd probably already heard. Like everybody else up the north coast, Rose was coming to know:

λ Grizzly bears sharpen their claws on the same tree for life, and like to step in their own prints, too, on their own paths, year after year.

λ You always dance north.

λ The lighthouse blew off Egg Island one bad night back in the twelve-dollars-a-ton herring reduction fishery days.

λ You need to be smarter than a duck to get one with a 410 shotgun, and even then, you need to "Indian up" on them.

λ The best jelly is made from salal berries, and no decent-size salal grows south of Port Neville.

λ You feed fresh-dug clams first to the cats, who let you know in a hurry if they're poisoned by red tide.

λ The pilchards will come back one day.

λ Pierre Trudeau's cousin was tie up man on one of those Masset seine boats last year.

λ Indian radar is kelp over the rocks, and Indian sonar is yelling off the cliff for an echo.

λ It's possible to live off the land or, let's say, out of the sea, if you have enough canned tomatoes, pilot biscuits, coffee and a case of Pacific milk on board. A stash of this stuff sits in old gear lockers somewhere if you run out. Probably in Bones Bay, or at Butedale, where that waterfall makes enough electricity to light the whole coast if you only knew how to plug it in.

人 Langara Deep in the fishing area called North of 54 is a grey whale graveyard.

人 The coffee cups on the boat need to hang facing inboard so as not to pour luck over the side.

人 No cans should be opened upside down for fear of overturning the boat.

人 A black suitcase brings a doctor, and maybe death, on board.

人 You shouldn't go ashore anywhere near Grief Point the other side of Queen Charlotte Sound.

人 *Annie Tuck*, built in Vancouver in 1919 for Josiah Babcock of Nitinat, B.C.; fifty-five feet long, forty-one gross tonnes, is still working, and crosses Queen Charlotte Sound so easy by herself in a gale that she'll live forever.

人 You can still make out as a copper bandit if you know where to look.

人 The words for someone who gets fired or laid off are: "He had to go down the road, packing his lunch bucket and talking to himself."

人 The only possible response to being fired is: "Fuck you. I was lookin' for a job when I found this one."

人 A transistor radio will play for a surprisingly long time underwater, if your name is Richard Bruce and you're eleven years old, leaning over the deck rail with your first radio, bought with your first fishing money, and you drop the radio gently, deliberately, into Rivers Inlet on a bright day.

Ⓝ That's Harry Assu's Cape Mudge seiner, *BCP 45*, loading up on sockeye in the 1958 bonanza year, right there on the back of the old five dollar bill. They should bring back that bill.

Ⓝ You throw the season's first sockeye bones back into the sea, where they'll continue their journey when the tide is right. Salmon don't like to buck tide.

Ⓝ Some days on some boats, fishing is just like being in jail with a better chance of drowning.

Ⓝ Freddy Edgar, late of Sunnyside Cannery on the Skeena River, the last man who knew the secret about the masks and coppers hidden on Aristazabal Island, has died and taken it with him.

Ⓝ Someone, preferably a grandmother, should bite off— never cut—a new baby's first fingernail growth.

Ⓝ A woman stepping across the net, or standing over it with her legs open, at least, is good luck at the start of the fishing season.

Ⓝ A mouthful of gasoline will kill the nerve in a painful tooth.

Ⓝ You don't need ammunition for a clam gun, because a clam gun is a pitchfork; and the real name for a shovel is Box #2 with a wooden beam.

Ⓝ Fort Rupert round steak is baloney, a tube steak is a weiner, and honey, well, it looks like honey, but it's not.

Ⓝ The boat recipe for liver is, "Fry the piss out of it, and chuck it overboard."

Ⓝ In hard, hard times, people up the coast have eaten wind

pudding and air pie.

⋏ When you dream of the dead, you should never eat any food or drink they offer you, or you'll have to go back with them.

⋏ A stone pillar rests in the sea under the blowhole at the mouth of Rivers Inlet.

⋏ Prince Rupert is the most perfect natural deepwater harbour in the world.

⋏ Wolves will come down on the beach and dig clams in a tough-enough winter.

⋏ Porch-climber is the real name for the red wine that comes in boxes.

⋏ Christmas day will never be exactly the same as it was before the *Lee Wang Zin*, carrying 54,000 tonnes of iron ore pellets, 372,000 gallons of fuel, and thirty men, turned turtle in hurricane force winds near Celestial Reef in Dixon Entrance on the morning of December 25, 1979.

⋏ A hunter's moon is no moon at all.

⋏ Cats and raccoons have been known to mate. Look at Bill, that black tom with the huge shoulder muscles in Double Bay who fishes the tide pools as good as any coon.

⋏ The last member of Butch Cassidy's and the Sundance Kid's gang died from hard Colt rain at the back of a cave near the Kluxewe River outside Port Hardy in the prospecting days.

⋏ The ghosts of children from Glen Vowell, Kispiox, Kitseguecla and Kitwanga on their way to the St. Albert residential school outside of Edmonton are still looking out the train windows along the Bulkley River.

Ꭹ Simon Gunanoot, trapping and travelling alone in the bush between Hazelton and the Yukon border, 1906 to 1919, on the run from bounty hunters, Pinkerton's men and the Provincial police, is still around and will appear with a quarter of venison and a light if you're lost out there. Ꭹ One of the travelling carnival ponies, roped to a wheel to walk in a small circle with children on their backs all day and into the night, got loose in Terrace. She's still out there in the bush somewhere along the Skeena.

Rose, and everyone else up the coast then, also knew it was true that certain boats aren't lost, no matter how long people searched and found nothing—no planks, no life rafts or rings, no radio message, no bodies. Those boats and their crews are still here on the coast. Somewhere. Up the head of Cumshewa Inlet living the good life maybe. In the Aleutians under different names.

Who knows who else might still be alive up the coast somewhere...Jimi Hendrix, installing Satnav systems and stereos on halibut longliners out of Cow Bay? Russian trader Aleksandr Baranof, organizing the building of another sailing ship called *The Phoenix*, made from mountain ash, caulked with native moss and hot pitch, in the Alaskan bay he named *Resurrection* on Easter Sunday, 1792? Or Captain Cook, his bones brought back from Hawaii to be clothed with flesh and pushed into life again by that famous Kitkatla shaman who was perfectly capable of sitting in the best place by the fire in the village, and keeping watch from the rock on the burial island at the same time? James Cook lives quietly now at the head of a bay the other side of Milbanke Sound, where the deer and the salmon and all needed creatures are still willing. This bay is so perfectly hidden from storms and other chaos Cook could never bear to chart or name it.

Reincarnation, or some second chance, can happen. Up the coast, there was a girl who from birth was the spit and spirit of her mother's dead sister. The small girl's astonishing needlework, and her love for her aunt's hand-wheel Singer sewing machine raised everyone's hopes. Then the wind roared in the child's ears and made her cry, long before anyone else knew her aunt's bones in the tree grave box had been storm-scattered.

More than her own cooking, the rich crumbs of these truths swelled Rose while Richard was away on the boat. Lillian, in Rupert for the day on her way to an Alcoholics Anonymous rally in Prince George, swore she was taller. Richard, home one night between herring openings, said he honestly thought her breasts were bigger.

Rose's territory was larger, too. In Alert Bay, she'd stayed put, recording salmon catch and river escapement statistics for Fisheries in the summers, embroidering chain stitch teal ocean waves on quilt tops in winter:

Bring your thread (two strands of the six strand embroidery floss available in a hundred colours at Bing Toy's store in the Bay) out at the required point. Re-insert the needle near the same point, leaving a small loop of thread free on the right side of your work. Bring the thread out again a tiny distance from the first point; catch the loop and pull it tight. The stitch is now complete. Re-insert your needle near the last point to begin the next stitch.

In Alert Bay, the sea moved, and Richard and the other men on boats moved with it, while Rose sat in safe harbour. But in the new north coast country, where the Department of Fisheries and Oceans stretched inland to the Nass and Skeena headwaters, the question most often asked on her first Fisheries jobs was, "Someone has to get wet and cold and dirty, Rose. Who's it gonna be?" Creek names and fish numbers slid out of their paper files to come alive under her wet hands and in the pools around her boots:

Diana Creek, Ecstall River, Prudhomme Creek, Shawatlan Creek, Clear, Dry and Goat creeks, Kasiks River, Nangeese River, Kitseguecla River, Kleanza Creek, Kloiya Creek, Telkwa River, Gitnadoix and Shegunia and Atna rivers, Big Falls and Big Useless and Hays creeks, Toon River and the Lachmach in Work Channel, Kincolith and Kiteen rivers and Ksedin Creek on the Nass.

Thread them down mountainsides, stitch them together in a pouring, joined pattern of water falling down the land into the Pacific. Rose never considered trying to photograph and print these moving waters into stillness.

She was safe up there, once she had become a woman who could stop on the Yellowhead Highway past Kitwanga to look up at Rocher de Boule Mountain, knowing she was Rose Bruce, whose husband had gone on the herring, who was on her way to a salmon enhancement meeting in Smithers, or to see Magdalena Naziel at Two Mile about cedar baskets for the museum. Knowing too, underneath this dailiness, that the mountain's real name was Stek-yaw-den, that the mountain goat whose head hung above the Cheezies in the Kitseguecla store was of the same nation as the goat whose hoof made the mountain tremble when he danced for the Tsimshians before anyone else was here. Remembering that the goats from these mountains lived incandescent incarnations in the 1850s, when the Hudson Bay fort at Port Simpson had to trade goods for goat tallow to make two thousand candles a year. Rose, on the edge of the Yellowhead Highway, is content to know that both Magdalena Naziel and the creeks to be spoken of at the salmon enhancement meeting contain secrets she will never learn. Her mind map of northwest British Columbia moving waters, salt and fresh, and the true stories marked on it, moisten dry ground.

The story of Rose's father's funeral is also true.

"His heart was tired. There's no more to it than that. Why do you keep fussing at me about it? Don't you have black shoes?" her mother says the day of the Requiem Mass at St. Stephen's, Kerrisdale, Vancouver, B.C.

First, St. Stephen gives Rose, "Good King Wenceslas last looked out on the Feast of Stephen." Then, he offers the fishermen's version:

Good King Wenceslas last looked out
wearing his pajamas.
What d'ya think was hanging out?
Peaches and banana.

Requiem comes from the Latin, to rest. But Rose, who will never make it up to her father now, is standing in St. Stephen's right front pew, steadying her red suede boots to brace against her mother's weight leaning on her shoulder, and focussing on Requiem—resting—sharks, not Requiem mass. These sharks, including Pacific—a.k.a. spiny—dogfish, are apt to appear in large numbers during restful, fair weather. Spiny dogfish are, at this moment, a comfort to Rose. Their desultory, little-known journies across the Pacific, or north and south along the coast, or from the surface to four hundred fathoms. Their oil, once used to fuel lighthouse beacons, is said to burn with a soft yellow glow and no stink.

But the dorsal fin spines on dogfish hurt your hands like héll as well as tear the net. Deck hands with the time and inclination yank dogfish snouts upwards, then chuck them overboard to swim in hopeless circles. To discourage them. Only it doesn't work. More dogfish come back in the next set or haul. They have a gestation period of twenty-two to twenty-four months. Two to twenty developing young are carried. There's evidence of abortion or miscarriage in dogfish populations. An average eight or nine live young are born. With turquoise eyes, Rose has noticed.

She inhales prayers: Glory be to the Father, and to the

Son and to the Holy Ghost, and the scent of the funeral wreaths with not a rose among them. It is necessary, then, to invoke another fish for an amulet against death and daughters who fail their fathers.

When they are lying on the deck about to die, Pacific halibut look as if they still have deepwater secrets to comfort them in this dry new world. One secret might be how easy it is to understand the weight and meaning of the lost ocean now that they are swimming in the air.

The serene sideways mouths of halibut say they have consented to be caught, have agreed to be gaffed, or shot with a .22 or left thrashing on the hatch cover minute after minute in the late afternoon. Their dappled skins, each coloured and patterned after the particular shadows of home, stay bright for hours past death. The possibilities of transcendence attend halibut even as they are opened and gutted. The albatrosses wheeling above the bloody decks offshore are known to be drowned halibut fishermen.

Richard says halibut come willingly to be caught if you call them by their secret name. The hook of memory is set in Rose's own mouth while she remembers green rain gear stretching across his back as he bends over the side of the skiff. His voice whispers into the dark water off Porcher Island. The line gulps urgently in his hands and the halibut comes up out of the sea looking like an overturned island, looking as if it will know its own name forever. Rose kneels beside her mother:

Hear my prayer, O Lord, and with thine ears consider my calling. Hold not thy peace at my tears, for I am a stranger with thee, and a sojourner, as all my fathers were.

O spare me a little, that I may recover my strength before I go hence, and be no more seen.

As it was in the beginning, is now, and ever shall be: world without end.

Amen

Rose extends whatever blessings have been evoked by Requiem sharks, Pacific halibut and Psalm 39 to Simon Peter Gunanoot, a man on the run in the bush, still alive, still free, after all these years. He's waiting for Rose in the woods the other side of Two Mile on the Yellowhead Highway past Moricetown in case she's ever desperate to escape. The benedictions also shelter Billy Macken, who is away, upcountry, right now, but who will return for Rose if she needs him, and Richard, who might be dead, for all Rose knows. He never responded to her radio message for the *Florentina* to call home after she heard from Jean next door on Arbutus Street about her father.

Richard's transmissions from the fishing grounds often consisted of silence, and now, after almost ten years, Rose has taken to imagining *Florentina* as a drifting overturned hull. She gets as far as shameful worries about marine salvage rights, and wondering if she should sit with the girls who belong to Richard's crewmen at the funerals. Or would the drownings somehow be partly her fault because she was Richard's wife, so she should sit by herself?

Richard might need St. Nicholas more than St. Stephen. Nicholas loves sailors, children and pawnbrokers.

A drowned man should lie at least a day before a statue of Nicholas, Greenlanders say, in case the saint makes a miracle for him. But Richard hasn't drowned. He's sitting in the captain's chair in the house in Prince Rupert, watching rain slash the window, waiting for Rose when she returns from her father's funeral.

"Come here, Rosie. I'm sorry, Sorry. Sorry." He has her on his lap now, is trying to rock her, wet raincoat and damp, wildly curling hair and all. But Rose will not be rocked. She's on her feet, wrenching off her coat, then kneeling in front of her husband.

"Rose, wait." One hand on her shoulder, one hand clutching the tangled hair to hold her head back.

When she's done, leaning back with her hands still out-stretched and her flushed cheeks glistening, with her skirt tumbled above her knees to show creamy lace and thighs and no panties, she won't let him into her.

"I got back soon as I could. Yesterday, early. Just missed you the night before. Do you want tea?" Richard, who hates tea, makes it the way Rose likes it—clear, pale, with a piece of lemon. "Tell me about it. How was your mother?"

"In charge. The way she is. She wouldn't even tell me herself on the phone. She got Jean next door to do it. So even if I got the plane from here, or went over to Sandspit and down, or whatever, I'd still be too late, or too early or in the wrong place at the wrong time to help."

A swooning candle flame and the steam rising from their teacups are the only movement in the room. Richard has turned out the overhead light and lit one of Rose's huge homemade candles (layers of crimson wax paling into blush pink, dyed with varying size chunks of lipstick, flavoured with cloves and oil of roses) to soften things for her. But Rose doesn't need softening. There are no tears.

"He looked at you all the time," Richard says. "He looked at you like he loved you."

Silence. The twisting of a lemon slice. Chink of a teaspoon. "How would you know? All you ever talked to him about was the difference between seining and gillnetting. The same question for nine years."

"He mentioned a river once, last time." Richard's wearing the closed patient look he assumes when accompanying Rose to the annual after-salmon season dinner with her parents in Vancouver. She hasn't earned this particular expression from him until now. The dinner evening is always cut short as soon as Rose has helped her mother with the dishes. She and Richard say they have to make the tide out of Celtic Shipyard near the mouth of the river, or get a taxi to the airport for Canadian Flight 560 to Terrace and Prince Rupert. But they are really going straight downtown to the Nelson Place Hotel on Granville, where all the fishermen go.

"Why was he talking about the Fraser River, or did he mean the Skeena?" Rose is hopeful. Perhaps she, represented by Richard while she was washing dishes, had been some kind of wild Rose of Canada in her father's eyes, after all. If he was talking about rivers, not taxes, he must have been thinking of her.

"Not rivers here. Some small river in the mountains there. Where he was born. He only said he remembered it."

But this secondhand memoir belonging to a boy she never knew, who grew up in Austria, where there is only supposed to be the Danube River, causes Rose to turn on the light and advance to the kitchen to make pastry for butter tarts the Alert Bay way.

Use half as much shortening as you have flour. Add a pinch of salt. With sharp, delicate motions, not wide, muddy strokes, mix in half as much very cold water as shortening. Fill the pastry-lined tart pans half to two-thirds full with a mixture of one beaten egg, one-third of a cup butter, one cup brown sugar, two tablespoons of milk, one-half of a cup currants and a teaspoon of vanilla. Bake.

After the butter tart night following her father's funeral, Rose is so restless she needs to walk back and forth in front of the Fisheries information desk in the basement of the Federal Building while she researches managers' briefing notes. The butter tart night was the beginning of Richard closing in on her, Rose figured out a long time afterward. He was home from fishing more often after that, even if it meant running in the dark.

Some nights, Richard says she feels so brittle under his hands her bones might snap and asks when she'll be pliable for him again. He never questioned Rose much, before. He didn't ask about the photographs he saw when they packed the moving boxes in Alert Bay. In those prints, the Bay was unrecognizable until it became clear Rose had flipped her negatives, so the curve of the beach set St. Michael's

Residential School where the graveyard should be, or altered perspective so murky water appeared to lie above sunken streets and docks. Some of the prints showed the houses on the hill behind the breakwater smudged into a dark forest on which Rose had scratched indecipherable marks.

Richard doesn't bring up those altered images now, or ask Rose why she never uses the darkroom cupboard he made for her beside the washing machine in the basement of the Beach Street house. He only asks, "What's this?" when he comes back from a Babine Lake moose trip, and finds a jean jacket crumpled on the floor behind his chair.

Rose, startled, says nothing at first. 'This' is an old Levi Strauss denim jacket, softened and frayed at cuffs and collar. Entirely desirable. Anyone would want it. "I found it," she says, finally, but Richard has already struggled into the jacket.

"Fits," he announces happily.

"It does not," Rose is screaming without sound. "It doesn't fit you at all." But Richard is searching the pockets, hoping perhaps (would he have been hoping? Rose at Roberson Point almost fifteen years later still wonders) that she had left some talisman of herself in the jacket's heart pocket, something to remind him of her when he's away. One of those beads the nuns make from rose petals would have been perfect.

Gather a shopping bag full of wild rose petals. Grind them in a hand grinder until they are as smooth as modelling clay. Store this rose matter in a cast-iron skillet and grind again every two weeks until it thickens. Roll bead-size bits between your hands until smooth. Put a pin through each bead and fasten it to a board, where it must dry for about two weeks, if you are a Russian, Serbian or Greek Orthodox sister in a monastery set under an inland sun, or if the sloping garden of the Catholic convent in the Tatra or Dolomite or Carpathian mountains is sheltered from early autumn wind by stone walls. The drying time for rose beads is much longer on the humid, heavy-aired north Pacific coast. Polish the finished beads with a soft cloth and string them on dark, heavy thread.

Even a spoonful of rose jam wrapped in a tiny foil packet could have travelled in that pocket. The jam would have been made from the recipe Rose convinced her mother to find in the letters from her own mother she used to say she'd thrown out.

Rosenblattgelee: Crush fresh rose petals into sugar syrup until the syrup can hold no more. Boil until the jam holds shape on a silver spoon. Bottle. The edges of the rose petals will appear to be glazed with light when you hold the jar up to the window.

This is the jam Rose held in her mouth, and in the hood of her clitoris, one night a long time ago, while Richard kissed her.

But Richard doesn't need a memento. He has the denim jacket now, and he's taken to bringing home more of the truth of what fishing is like for him, so he must remember his wife of his own accord when he's on the boat.

"Sometimes I just know," he says, trying to explain to Rose, who hasn't asked him, how you know where to try your net underneath that rippling or heaving surface that never bears any signs saying, Fish Here.

"Not always." Rose already knows he isn't invincible because he sometimes comes back from fishing with nothing to say about anything.

"I mean, there's the tide, and the feed, and rain or no rain, or whether they're waiting to go up." He can at least take it for granted by now that Rose will know "they" are salmon, waiting to rush up their home rivers to spawn.

"Or if the herring are close to spawning, or still roaming around. And what they did last year, or five years ago. But sometimes I just know."

Here's Richard, before herring season in March, safe in his bed in the Prince Rupert house, with Rose who has been turned and opened, naked and sleepy beside him. He's wide awake. "I get scared, Rosie, sometimes. Coming around Cape Scott last time I left the net on the drum. The guys were tired. We could have rolled a couple of times. Stupid. I didn't used to get scared when it wasn't my boat. When I was on the crew with the old man, I mean. You know."

Rose imagines she does know. John Bruce would have sucked up any fear that showed its face on his boat, and spat it out his wheelhouse window.

Richard's on a roll now, sitting up in bed, lighting a smoke. "I get sick of the radio. Nobody ever shuts up out there. I'm fuckin' sick of telling lies on Channel 78, and getting them back from other guys." Rose props herself on her elbows to lean into him and soften his anger with her skin. But, no. "And I hate always pushin' some other guy for a set, or getting pushed. There's more pricks fishing than there used to be."

Rose, sitting up with her eyes wide open now too, plumps the pillows for both of them, but finds nothing to say except, "The *Florentina*'s a good boat, though, isn't she?"

"If she could do her own paperwork, and make herself invisible to the Fisheries plane, she'd be even better." Richard gives his cigarette stub an overboard flick, then watches it bounce off the wall and burn on the floor for a second or two before he rolls out of bed to reach for it. "Yeah, Rose, she's a good enough boat. I just gotta live up to her is all."

A week later, Richard calls Rose from the pay phone in Namu to tell her a story called This is What Happened to the *Ocean Provider*:

They crossed the Sound with the Silver Moon. *Gusting seventy. Green water over the cabins. The skiff blew off the* Provider's *deck, then the stabilizers went. The crew was in the wheelhouse on both boats, crowded up, I guess, laughing, fooling around on the radio. One guy on the* Provider, *he says, 'You guys got any coffee over there? Our big pot and all the cups're smashed on the galley floor.' Then the* Provider *captain, he says on the radio, 'I can feel my mouth getting dry,' and she's gone.* Silver Moon *couldn't turn. In that sea."*

This time, when Richard gets back and is awake in the night, Rose asks him to tell her What Happened to the *Ocean Provider* again. He repeats the story in the same words, adding only at the end, "*Silver Moon* bought a case of rye in Namu."

By May, when everyone has salmon fever, and Richard is spending his days hanging his net to mend web in B.C. Packers' netloft at Port Edward, he's leaning over his beer at the Oceanview or the Empress, trying to tell Rose, fast, before someone comes over, or Tom sings again, how Fishing is Life. "I know how to do it," or "I started with John when I was just a kid," is where he begins. Sometimes, after four or ten beers, he says, "It's like home, Rose."

Once, after Tom at the Empress sang Stan Rogers' "The *Jeannie C.*," Richard tells Rose, "When I come in, even if I'm happy as hell to be off the boat because it's been haywire out there, I still kind of feel sorry for everyone in town who missed everything. Even you."

Rose feels the same every time she drives the last hundred kilometres along the Skeena back to Rupert at dusk, tired, watching the curves and counting the Skeena streams like rosary beads, or when she gets off the Cessna from Kitkatla or Ketchikan, or the Fisheries boat after a skim up the west coast of the Charlottes to the Port Louis and Port Chanal streams running in woods so old and deep their breath stirs the air. But she tells Richard nothing. Aren't these things supposed to be a secret?

In the kitchen on a Saturday morning after the first

northern salmon seine opening, Richard, in a shy voice she's never heard from him before, tells Rose he thinks he's ready for a child.

Rose, at this moment, is struggling with the black cast iron frying pan she has, as usual, been too impatient to heat up enough for French toast. The soggy bread just sits there, slowly soldering itself to the pan. Rose knows the secret of decent French toast too, from Lillian:

Set the bread into the egg and milk mixture the night before. Use a drop of vanilla and a toss of cinnamon instead of sugar. Hide that vanilla now unless you want to make 'niller punch at the end of a hard winter, the way the east coasters used to do.

And there can be no baby from Rose, no small Rose, either boy or girl. None, none at all. The baby would have a problem and she would never know what to do. She would be the problem, the disappointment. Or the baby would be a disappointment. It would be disappointed with her.

Richard, manfully eating his scraped-up-out-of-the-frying-pan French toast: "I might sell the *Florentina* after the season if I can get into something smaller with no loan. Cod boat, maybe. Be home more."

Rose, not eating, smoking one of Richard's Rothman's, whispering, " I never knew you wanted a baby."

"Most people do, sooner or later. Don't you?" A pause. "What do you want, Rose?"

Nothing. Wrapped in an apricot silk quilt with ravaged, butter yellow borders, and sitting across the table from him, she's already gone, riding the muddy highwater scent of the river that has flowed into the kitchen. The river water is milky with silt, spiked with uprooted stumps and deadfall trees, and moving fast enough to carry the weight of one woman. The blue cable drum table, still stencilled Wire Rope Industries, and the quilt, will have to stay behind.

Richard's going down to the *Florentina* at B.C. Packers' floats now, as soon as he kisses his wife on the cheek and puts on his new, old denim jacket. But Rose is going away. Not immediately, but after one more trip to the fish ladder at the junction of the Nass and Meziadin rivers, and one more drive back to Prince Rupert along the Skeena, after one more walk up the hill in Port Simpson to look out at Rose Island. After the salmon season and this Fisheries contract are finished. After none of the things she ought to have done are left undone, except for being a wife.

Down Here In the City

*R*ose, drinking coffee out of a steel Thermos lid while her back rests against a fir stump next to the petroglyph, can admit, at least to herself and the stone woman the other side of the stump, that Richard thought he might find her, all of her, when he came out of hiding himself. Rose, holding on to the fir roots stretching twice her height beside her, still thinks she could have done nothing else but run, then. Richard had broken their unspoken bargain that he would always be a pirate who didn't ask hard questions. She would need to be her own pirate then. The journey is the thing. A moving target is harder to hit.

He didn't try to persuade her to stay, and he was passed out on the couch when she left. Rose thought his face looked as shuttered and blank as it had the first time he handed her onto his boat at the Campbell Avenue dock in Vancouver. She stood over Richard tilting her head forward and back, side to side, trying to remember the best angle for a resting neck so she could arrange him as if he were sleeping. But translation from her body to Richard's had become impossible.

She filled fishermen's luggage (green garbage bags) with clothes from one extreme (grey wool work socks, flannel shirts, jeans and fish-scaled boots) to the other (a navy blue sweetheart-neck 1930s silk crepe from the Salvation Army thrift shop on Third, a certain successfully iridescent copper beaded sweater, the Port Essington lace curtain scrap often used as a scarf, and two identical shoplifted black lace bras, the first nipped up Richard's sleeve with ease, the second, which took weeks of gearing up to achieve, stolen by Rose to keep pace.) Middle ground office clothes were left behind. The sketchbooks and the Pentax were stuffed into the garbage bags without much care. Spare-time attempts at art didn't matter that night.

While the *Queen of the North* steamed past Barrett Rock Light and twelve more hours of night coast, Rose had time to regret going down to the Drifter Hotel to sell the Remington 410 over-and-under shotgun before she left. Richard gave it to her two Christmases ago. He said it would last a lifetime if she looked after it. Probably true. A lifetime owned by a thin guy down from Granduc Mine who bought himself a bargain brand light shotgun and .22 together.

A gillnetter named Tommy Jack laid a school of northbound matchstick sockeye on her table in the ferry's bar. She had time to figure out which four wooden match fins to move to make them swim south.

Around one in the morning, another passenger told her about a murder he'd had to do "because there was no other way." He wasn't caught and the log boom eventually sold anyway for a not bad dollar. The hours until morning in Queen Charlotte Sound were time enough for Rose to convince herself he had chosen her as a confidante because he thought she would have done the same thing in his place. Fear and flight must show on your face. Probably in the eyes. Rose went into the main deck washroom to look at her face, sliding around the mirror in a 4.6-metre sea off Egg Island Light, to prove her eyes were the same changeable grey as the murderer's. She entered his story, a reverberation of her own cloudy guilt, onto the list of what is known to be true up the coast.

Between the Vancouver Island ferry terminal in Port Hardy and the Nimpkish River bridge, Rose wondered if you could still see directly across Johnstone Strait to Alert Bay, from the middle of the bridge, if there are no logging trucks: yes.

From the mid-island ferry terminal in Nanaimo, across Georgia Strait to Vancouver, she wondered if she would be allowed to survive the city again by living on the Sandheads lightship at the mouth of the Fraser, or on the lighthouse under Lions Gate Bridge: no.

Rose found a room, $275 a month, on Wall Street, where she could almost see grain ships loading at the elevator, and could easily walk along the waterfront as far as the cottage called The Flying Angel Mission to Seamen, marooned at the container port gate. She waited for lights on street corners, wondering how the winter was going for the wolverine who stood up on his hind legs to mutter a warning across fifty metres of Morice Lake ice last year.

She got a job teaching photography with six donated, crashed up 35 mm cameras two nights a week for Carnegie Centre at Hastings and Main on the downtown east side. After taking portraits of her students with the program coordinator's Polaroid, she proceeded to printing their *Views of Home*, the first and only assignment. There were smiles, sometimes cropped to exclude identifying features; hands holding each other, or reaching out to other hands, or fisted or cupped to receive, and steep staircases up to curtained Keefer Street windows containing geraniums. The harbour three blocks north never appeared in any of the photographs. James, ancient mariner, merchant kind, who came faithfully to every class, took four rolls of the Ovaltine Café, on East Hastings, at night. Steamed windows from every f-stop around the dial shone softly into rain-slicked neon nights and dawns.

"What'll we call these?" Rose asked him once she realized she had probably been given the teaching contract because she looked as much in need of a second chance as anyone in the class. Now she was determined that a sample of every student's work would be matted, titled and exhibited on Carnegie's third floor walls. James's best Ovaltine Café prints were mounted as *Night Hoping 1,2,3,& 4,* and Rose, in the Sally Ann silk crêpe, started going to Arbutus Street on Sundays again, to tell stories to her mother.

One Sunday, Rose's mother says, "If you read it in a book, you'd never believe it," after Rose tells her a story about something that really happened to someone she knew up the coast. Rose's stories never take place in

Vancouver. They usually show that hard times, or courage, or love, or some question about all three are on Rose's mind. The people in the stories don't fit comfortably around her mother's polished fruitwood table, scattered with sherry glasses on Sunday afternoons.

"You do it deliberately," Rose's mother says, frowning at a bowl of pink and red tulips on the mantelpiece. "Are those tulips past it? It's probably too warm for them in here."

"Do I?" Rose asks. But she knows she does. To remind herself she's not the only one out of place in this ordered house, Rose surrounds her mother's table with companions from wilder regions.

Rose, for example, has told her mother the story of a woman she knows who lived in a floathouse in Simoom Sound behind Alert Bay, years ago, mind you, but still. She's cooking in a logging camp and one night her door flies open in the the dark and in come two loggers carrying a boy. He's maybe twenty, only been in camp a couple of days and he's bleeding all over her floor from cuts on his neck and arm and a deep wound in his thigh. The fight doesn't matter to the story because they lay him down and he soaks her couch before she can bind him up with the first-aid kit bandages.

The bandages run out so she starts using towels and sheets and yelling at the loggers to get ice from the freezer. She uses up the ice and has to pack frozen pork roasts and most of the deer the faller shot last week alongside the boy. The bleeding from his neck slows down and his arm is OK, but blood still wells from his leg no matter how tightly she twists the sheets.

It's past midnight now and the boy is pale and hasn't said anything for a long time. The floathouse is crashing around and the wind won't drop until morning. One of the loggers is back in the bunkhouse and the other is asleep in a chair while the woman bends over the boy, trying to trickle sugared tea into his mouth. His arm is propped on a pile of clean sheets, and she's thinking, God forbid, that tomorrow is clean laundry day in the bunkhouse.

At three in the morning, the boy is still. She's so tired of wrapping the top half of him with blankets while she raises his leg, then lowers it to tighten and loosen the sheet soaking with blood, that she falls asleep. For how long she doesn't know. When she wakes up, she's sure he's dead. She jumps up and goes to the cupboard. Rose imagines her walking stiffly, looking as if she knows exactly what she's doing. She gets one of the thick white coffee cups and goes back to the boy, unwinds the sheet stiffened and heavy with blood and reveals the wound. She presses the coffee cup into his slashed flesh and blood slides down the side of the cup. When the bottom of the cup is covered, she ties the last sheet around the leg and goes to the stove. She fills the cup with hot water from the kettle and adds an Oxo cube.

Rose wonders, if it's the combination of an ordinary Oxo cube with the mystery of the blood that makes her mother so angry when she tells her about the woman in Simoom Sound.

The woman marches (Rose always sees her marching)

over to the boy she thinks is dead, or so close it doesn't matter. She tilts his head back roughly—she said herself she wasn't gentle at this point—pinches his nose, and pours the contents of the cup down his throat. Most of it comes up, but some goes down. She only does it once. The plane comes in the morning and at St. George's Hospital in Alert Bay they pump blood into him for two days. For years after that, the boy writes to the Simoom Sound woman on his birthday. Rose has seen the letters. The last one came from Fort McMurray. The woman never told the boy, or anyone else, about the cup of blood until she told Rose.

Rose is satisfied with everything about this story. It all really happened. If she believes the facts of it, she has to accept the questions too. What made the woman give him his own blood, and did it make any difference and why did she keep it secret? If her mother read about the woman from Simoom Sound in a book and didn't have to know she was real, she wouldn't mind so much, Rose thinks. Comfort in the world must be a matter of what you decide is true.

When Rose lived in Alert Bay and Prince Rupert, her mother sent her new books once or twice a year. "So you remember the real life," her note might say. Or, "So you will think, still! Love, Mother." The books were almost always novels and short stories about women who thought deeply about their unsatisfactory lives, then changed them.

But, "You read too much," Richard used to say. "It's not the real world." Meaning, Rose guesses, "Books are only paper moons." He might be right, about the reading at least. Fiction can't help her now. Perhaps her mother thinks so too. These days she gives Rose photocopies of articles about late bloomers' career chances, and divorce settlements, and suggests she should make notes when she gets back to Wall Street.

Rose rubs neat's-foot oil into her old boots for a long time before she does this. She slides down in her chair, props her booted feet on the table and reads, "Revised divorce laws in British Columbia mean that all property accumulated during a marriage will be divided between both partners on the dissolution of the marriage." In the margin of the article she sketches a tiny *Florentina*, complete with cabin and seine drum, then draws a line bisecting the boat from bow to stern.

She remembers a story, second-hand and from long ago, about another couple who went their separate ways. The old man who told it to her must have been a boy when Sing got on the train with him at Hazelton sometime in the 1920s.

Sing (he was old himself, then) sits by the train window, staring out. A stretch of the Skeena River goes by while the boy is wondering how far downriver Prince Rupert will be, then he asks the old Chinese man where he's going.

A long time ago, more than fifty years ago, Sing tells him, he was in the Cariboo looking for gold. But he's too late. He hears news of gold on Manson Creek though, far to the north. So he buys a mule and some grub and gear (an outfit, he calls it) and walks to Manson Creek.

Rose is recalling the start of this story more carefully

than she usually does (it's the end she favours) and she frowns, knowing that the man who told her the story, and she herself, take walking to Manson Creek for granted. That is, with the respect the trail over mountains and rivers and through the bush, and the man who made the journey, deserve. Some people, Rose thinks, will not understand even this much about the story.

When Sing gets to Manson Creek, he finds gold. A government man named Billy Steel registers his claim. Winter's coming on and people tell him how hard and cold it's going to be, maybe forty below. He cuts a lot of wood and gets through the winter, though it's just as bad as everyone says. In the spring he starts mining again, and it's hard to work all day, then cut wood and cook. So he walks the trail to Fort Babine.

Rose can't figure this out, not on a modern map anyway. How did he cross Takla Lake? Why not go down to Fort St. James? When she remembers this part of the story, she mourns briefly that she's come so close to Manson Creek and not seen it. She's been to Fort St. James, along Stuart and Trembleur lakes and to Takla Landing, but not to Manson Creek. She knows gold was discovered on the Omineca River in 1871 though, and that Manson Creek flows into the Omineca.

At Fort Babine, Sing gets what he calls, in Chinook trade language, a "klootch" (a woman), a Carrier Indian woman called Emma. Emma is a good woman. "A damn good woman," Sing says, and the man who told Rose the story repeated it, and now Rose always does too when she tells the story.

Emma not only cuts wood and cooks and keeps the cabin clean, she works in the mine. Sometimes she runs a trapline and packs furs into the Fort for grub.

Sing and Emma live in this way for many years, very many years, and all is well. Then comes the winter when they are both old and there is silence between them for days. At last Emma says, "I know you want to go to China and die. I want to stay in the Babine country and die." And they are silent again.

Sing goes to the bank, he says, and gets out the gold dust and nuggets and dumps them onto a buckskin. He takes a stick and divides the pile of gold in half, then Emma sews the buckskin into little bags to hold the gold for both of them.

Sing and Emma walk the trail to Fort Babine where he leaves her, then he takes the other trail out to Hazelton and the train. Sing mentions the government's eternal promises to build a road instead of a trail out from the Fort, which makes the old man who told Rose this story laugh, and Rose too. She was on the Fort Babine road, gravelled now at least, just last year, photographing a salmon enhancement project. Sing will take the Union steamship from Prince Rupert to Victoria, then an Empress boat to China. The boy listening to his story on the train so long ago has two questions.

"Was Emma really your wife?" he asks.

Sing answers, "Fifty years in the same house with a good woman, that's a wife, even if there was no preacher."

And when the boy asks, "Was there really a bank up there?" Sing laughs.

"I dug a hole in the bank when I first come to Manson Creek. Covered it with mud and brush and no one found it in fifty years."

"You believe everything you want to believe," Rose's mother has said more than once, after her daughter has stumbled through some tale that proves the fluid, mysterious world can't be organized into immutability. No, Rose thinks, she isn't even sure any more what she needs to believe. She decides not to tell Sing's and Emma's story to her mother, no matter how long Sunday afternoon lasts. She would be angry knowing Rose is remembering those two managing the end of their life together with sorrow and grace, instead of concentrating on her own property settlement.

Does she even have a story her mother would want to believe, Rose wonders while she's folding the divorce article into a coaster and filling the kettle for tea. The third cup of tea is cold before the silver bracelet story comes back to her. Yes. Maybe this one.

Elizabeth Spalding has worn the bracelet on her left arm for seventy years, and her mother wore it before that. It shines softly against the blurred blue flowers on the tablecloth and chimes on the teapot when Elizabeth fills Rose's cup. The inner curve of the bracelet is dented and the wings of the eagle carving are nearly worn away.

Elizabeth is twelve, going to work in the Cassiar cannery for the first time, the summer her mother gives her the bracelet. Rose imagines her, small and straight-backed, sitting in an open boat from Port Essington, crossing the Skeena at slack water. Her right hand curves over the bracelet.

When the season is over and the salmon are done, Eddie comes to take Elizabeth to Port Simpson to help with her aunt's new baby. The wind blows strong southeast off Jap Point and Eddie's little boat rolls wildly. Elizabeth leans out to refasten the wheelhouse door, stumbles, then slides down the narrow, tilted deck into the sea. The bracelet, loose on the thin arm, catches on a cleat, holds long enough for Eddie to sweep her back. Her shoulder is wrenched and still gives her trouble all this time afterward. There's lots of snow and a long winter in Port Simpson, but the baby, a boy, gets fat, and Christmas is a good time with all the singing. It's flat calm all the way to Prince Rupert and up the river when Eddie takes Elizabeth back to her mother at Easter.

Even though silver whales circle her own wrist, Rose has forgotten Elizabeth Spalding's bracelet story for so long, that it doesn't ring familiar to her now. But like the Simoom Sound woman, and Sing and Emma on Manson Creek, like a daughter at her mother's table remembering other, more easily known places and people, Elizabeth and the bracelet her mother gave her are necessary to Rose in the city.

Some nights, Rose sits beside the phone on the floor in the Wall Street room, daydreaming up a man from the summer in Edmonton a year before she met Richard. Joe DesJarlais picked her up in front of the Bay on Jasper

Avenue every time she had a bad day stocking shelves in there. His car was old, floated along like a boat, gave off a smell of clean dust and gas she still missed. They did a lot of time in that car. Rose always wanted to drive as far north as you can go in one night and get back by morning: Fort Saskatchewan, St. Albert, Smokey Lake, Athabasca in the dark. And the Calling River, because she liked the name, but the water only sounded halting and slow, even in spring flood. Hundreds of miles together without saying much, and all the windows open. White line fever, Joe said she had. But in Alberta, it was easier to sleep in the car, waking to see the red glow of his cigarette moving slowly from his mouth to the ashtray and back, the country still slipping past black windows.

Rose made him take her all the way to Lloydminster just because she wanted to say she'd been to Saskatchewan. Sitting on the floor in Vancouver with the phone in her lap, she thought she'd been a dumb bitch, even then. Joe never said. He used to smile about her clothes: short skirts and her mother's desperate Peter Pan collared blouses. Later in the summer she bought a high-waisted, bright green cotton dress with tiny blue flowers. It soaked through in the rain after a thunderstorm one afternoon, outlining her body so she had to walk home looking into the distance, pretending not to notice. The dress was from Eaton's. Rose never bought clothes at the Bay, only stole *Beautiful Losers* and other books there on her lunch hour—her version of the employee discount. Joe wouldn't have believed her if she'd told him this. He said she shouldn't wear the same dress two days in a row because of what they would say about her at the Bay. She laughed, but he was right.

Sometimes he picked the places where they drove. They travelled slower then. There was a road through the fields outside of Wetaskiwin, narrow and feeling secret because the corn was neck-high by midsummer. Joe stopped the car in the middle of that road, then reached out for Rose, who ended up sprawled across the front seat underneath him. His shirt smelled like Sunlight soap. His dark hair was finer than her own. She laughed. She didn't know why, even more than ten years later. Joe just lay quiet, holding her down, until she started to wonder what would happen. But he let her go, and drove until the lights from the city showed up again over a rise in the road. In Alberta, Rose never got over expecting the sea to be there, waiting, on the other side of a dip in the road.

She didn't think he'd come back after Wetaskiwin, but he did. Saturday this time, because she wanted to see an oil rig like the one he worked on. But half an acre of dust and gravel and the clatter of the pump's downward thrust, followed up with the grittier backstroke, couldn't drown out Rose saying "No" when he got out of the car with her. The men on the rig were looking her over, and she didn't need Joe. He got back into the car to wait, and she walked over to the rig by herself. From the drilling platform, she saw him watching for a long time. She didn't look to see if he was still there when she got into the truck with the crew after their shift. They kept her with them in their trailer, drinking beer, and they never did jump her, but it seemed close for a while.

Rose didn't let herself get scared until three of them were driving her back to town. She jumped out of the truck at Jasper and Fifth and ran until she got to the apartment and saw herself in the mirror, white dust powdering her jeans and the pink shirt she never wore again, and big eyes staring out. She turned on the radio to make things ordinary and the news said a man (it sounded like DesJarlais) fired a gun on a street downtown, then shot himself. But the phone rang right away and Joe's voice shook with anger and fear, saying, "I guess you can look after yourself, right?" before he hung up.

She never did have Joseph DesJarlais's address. Before she left Edmonton to go back to school, she'd already lost the phone number for messages asking him to rescue her from parties that didn't work out, or bars on the south side.

It wasn't forgiveness for the oil rig day that had Rose calling from Wall Street in Vancouver to every DesJarlais in Alberta, and considering Saskatchewan and Manitoba. The last time Joe came to find her after work, he didn't wait in the car. He took hold of her arm on Jasper Avenue, turned her around to look into his face, and said, "Give me a chance, Rose. I can change. You'll see."

In the Wall Street room, she tried to think what he might be doing now. Sitting in the bar in Leduc. Talking to his children. The Beaufort drilling could have started up again. Or maybe he was building a house in Slave Lake. She hoped for these things. All this time, she'd been thinking Joe DesJarlais would find her again himself. So she could tell him, no one should promise to change. No one.

The last time Rose saw Richard in Vancouver, the salt water and diesel smell of his jacket gave the north coast back to her for an instant, then the waitress in a black dress smiled at him as if she were giving a party and was glad he'd come. The refuge coast retreated. The Howe Street piano bar returned.

Rose took off her bracelet to balance the semicircle of carved whale designs upside down on the table, then prodded the bracelet until the heads and tails rocked urgently from side to side. When the waitress left, she let the whales lie still. "Where did they find Johnny?" she asked.

Richard had turned away from her to watch men and women in smooth dark clothes hurrying to fill up the tables around them. He had managed to say that he was handlining cod around the Bay. He'd pushed a Rothmans package stuffed with fifties into her jacket pocket as an advance on her accumulated-since-marriage, minus bank loan payments, portion of the *Florentina* (about the size of that bunk below the waterline, plus a seat at the galley table, Rose figured). "About the same as the net share," Richard said, "and I get to keep the net." But he was grinning, so she could smile too. "There'll be more. Salmon will still be there when I get back into seining. Insaning." Rose waited. He'd already said his father had shot himself, but he might never tell her what she needed to know about where and how and why it happened.

"Alert Bay," Richard said. "The house by the breakwater." The waitress stood close to him when she returned with his beer and the red wine, Rose noticed. She needed both hands to lift the wine glass to her mouth, and still it danced against her teeth. Richard was twisted around in his chair again, surveying the crowd. "Rose," his voice floated back to her, "John was sick. He couldn't stay by himself in the floathouse in whatever out-of-the-way channel he wanted anymore."

Rose stopped herself from asking questions like, "Did he use his own shotgun? Did he leave a note?"

"If he was living in Alert Bay, what happened to his floathouse?"

"Gave it away, I guess. Same as he did with the boat back when he quit salmon fishing."

"His halibut licence?"

Richard shrugged. "That was a long time ago."

"Remember when we went into Freshwater Bay to see him?"

"He was never in Freshwater Bay."

Rose imagined herself lying adrift on the thin current of cool, exhaust-laden air entering the bar with each new arrival. Rolling slowly, she would be, crashing softly into bodies, trays, bar stools, moving back and forth on an air tide.

"He had his floathouse in Baronet Pass by the old mill when you were around Alert Bay, Rose." Richard set down his beer so he could use his forefinger to outline the Pass on the table.

Freshwater Bay was still a beautiful name, Rose assured herself. John Bruce could have, should have, tied his floathouse in there. She drank the last of her wine knowing Richard was never wrong about things like Baronet Pass and Freshwater Bay. He remembered twenty-year-old storms and the running time to everywhere on the coast. He used to forget to call home from the boat, but he remembered everything else. Rose centred her wine glass precisely on its coaster.

"What was he up to lately?" Her voice sounded sharp to her own ears, but who was more used to that than Richard? The waitress was back, smiling at him again. He ordered more drinks.

"Nothing" he said. "Living." Then, "You never used to ask about him from one year's end to the next, Rose. You hardly knew him."

She was suddenly so tired she wanted to fall forward and rest her head on the table. Impossible to explain that she needed to remember the coast perfectly down here in the city. Everything about how it had been up there was necessary, including Richard's father in his floathouse, being alone and tough and happy, not old and sick, not dead for God's sake. "When did you see him last?" she asked.

"In the café a week ago."

Rose shook her head. No. Johnny had no use for sitting around the café. Never. He would rather be whistling to call deer on the beach. Firing up his speedboat to go along the creek mouths to see if the last dog salmon had gone up, or shutting down the outboard on the way back in the dark to hear the wolves howling out of the inlets. The last time

Richard brought the boat that looked like *Florentina*'s daughter to Vancouver, Rose went to the False Creek dock to hear what was happening: copper rockfish on new grounds; cod prices up; Richard's dad alongside in his speedboat at dawn the week before. Richard said he yelled up, "Jesus Christ it's cold," and his hands were too numb at first to take hold of the lines to haul himself on board. There was a bottle in his jacket to spike the coffee. On his second cup, he told Richard he should get into the cod hole further north, and he marked it on the chart. He said that cod hole would be his legacy to Richard.

Rose looked past the crowded tables around them to the floor-length curtains shutting out the street, wondering if anyone else ever wanted to open a window in downtown bars. She tried to imagine John Bruce on land, in a house beside the breakwater in Alert Bay, or walking down the road to the café.

Richard leaned toward her. "When I saw him in the café, he said he needed a new hearing aid. His dog ate the first one."

Rose ignored him. Hearing aids and dogs had nothing to do with needing Johnny alive in his floathouse with the water and the beach and the trees around him the way they'd always been. Rose drained her glass and began another. Something old, something new. Something borrowed, something blue. Something lost. The wind blows. The dogs bark. The caravan moves on. Sometimes moves on, Rose whispered to the expectant silence inside her head. Sometimes the caravan moves on.

She tilted her glass too soon and wine pooled on the table. Never drink this much without eating, she told herself severely. Almost nothing was surprising any more, she decided. Not surprising to be alone. Not surprising to be in Vancouver instead of on the real coast. Everything changes. The inlets, bays, channels and islands up the coast might have altered their places and shapes and currents for all Rose knew, now that she was no longer there among them. She set down her glass.

Richard put a napkin over the puddle of wine. "Johnny was part Hawaiian," he said. "I never knew my grandmother, but she told him when he was a kid."

Rose reminded herself that Johnny had been Richard's father. Part Indian. Part something from Europe. Now, Richard was telling her John and he were somehow Hawaiian, too. She folded her hands together and sat up straight.

"Hawaiian sailors were making 'Pineapple Indians' around Alert Bay a hundred years ago." Richard looked at Rose. She managed a nod. "John said his mother used to talk about taking him to Hawaii. She drowned right out here in front." He gestured widely toward the entrance of the bar.

Rose clenched her hands together, and looked at the door to Howe Street. "Not here." Richard was impatient now. "In Johnstone Strait. In front of Alert Bay. She was out by herself when the wind came up. Her canoe washed back onto the beach, but they never found her body."

A piece of the land abandoning you, Rose thought. She

would have kicked hard and reached out, and the solidity of the cedar hull, surely still retaining some of the earth's warmth, would have slanted away beyond reach, leaving her alone in a fluid world that would bear her up for a while, then take her into itself.

"I hid in his bunk once, to see if he would miss me." Richard talked into his beer so Rose had to lean forward to hear him. "Running up north one summer when I was a kid. Small. One of the crew found me in there. I just wanted him, Johnny, I mean, to look at me." Silence. "He said he was tired, Rose. He didn't want to be sick any more. All he wanted to do was get to Hawaii."

Rose swallowed the last of her wine and tried to imagine Hawaii. Palm trees and white sand in the sun. Warm, sweet air tasting of flowers. The sea easy all the time, not grey and mean, the way it was here so much; only gently rocking, like a mother. Never a sign of nets or lines or any other work gear. No storms. No need to push yourself to leave safe harbours.

Richard shifted restlessly in his chair and Rose, watching him, understood that he wanted to leave because he had finished giving her the gift of answered questions about his father's suicide. He might have seen John looking at her once in a while when she was still his daughter-in-law, and just never said anything. Richard might even have known that his father called her Rambling Rose sometimes, when no one else was in the room or the galley or at the bar table. Only laughing a little, looking at her as if he knew her to the bone, and asking, "Ramblin' Rose, where the wind blows?" and not explaining except to tell her Nat King Cole sang "Rambling Rose." Richard was braver than she was, Rose thought, answering questions. The answers must be a kind of love, not what it had once been, but stubborn still, not drifting entirely out of sight.

On the street, she stood unsteadily beside him in the rain while he waited for a cab. He looked up at the night sky. "Supposed to blow southeast tomorrow." The taxi honked and he was gone.

Rose decided not to wonder if John Bruce had ever wanted to marry again, or to name to herself places up the coast where it would matter when the wind changed tomorrow. She walked with her arms slightly lifted to keep her balance, seeing that the rain and the wine were softening the edges of buildings and cars and lights, changing them into shapes that seemed new and already known at the same time, she thought, making the city easier to navigate.

At home on Wall Street, she ran a bath. The only photos from this time are self-portraits of Rose lying in the high-sided and claw-footed white tub. In these colour pictures, she's all angles again: chin, ribs, hips and knees surfacing like reefs from the bathwater. Even her breasts look sharp. The only curved line on Rose's body is the rise of soaked hair over soft flesh at the bottom of her belly. Although you can't tell from the photographs, the bathwater is moving, lapping Rose's body with small waves as she rocks her shoulders up and down without realizing what she's doing. Efforts to encourage rain to blow in the open window over the towel rack and sprinkle Rose, warm in the bath, have not been successful. All that comes in the bathroom window are wind and the wail of a train in the waterfront rail yard past Rogers Sugar.

> *There's a cunt on the track*
> *lets the train up her crack.*
> *She just wanted to get done.*
> *Now she's good and dead and gone.*
> —Rose Bachmann Bruce

The box on the 3/4 ton pickup bounced around when it was empty, and often enough, the gut truck was coming the other way. So Rose, by the grace of God, was going so slowly on the narrow, winding green-arched Skeena Slough Road with the river and the train tracks on the right that she stopped a good truck length in front of the woman who had laid herself down on the tracks with her head right where the truck's wheels would have been. Rose, leaning the truck door open, looked, absurdly, up to the left, where thick greenery and groundwater streams ran down the mountain. On this slanted green ground, upcountry children whose parents worked at Cassiar, Sunnyside and North Pacific canneries, used to play all summer. The longest manilla rope swing Rose has ever flown on is still tied to a huge cottonwood tree further along the road. Mildred Roberts, Elizabeth Spalding's niece, told her the mothers sometimes came out to the woods toward dusk after their cannery shift, calling, softly, "Simon...Simon Gunanoot..." just in case that man on the move with money on his head had made it through the bush this far to the coast. He might have needed a pan of hot rolls or somesuch.

"Simon Peter Gunanoot stands charged that he did at Hazelton-Aldermere Road, near Hazelton, in the County of Atlin and Province of British Columbia, on the 19th day of June, in the year of our Lord one thousand nine hundred and six, unlawfully kill and murder one Alexander MacIntosh against the Peace of Our Lord the King, his Crown and Dignity."

The clerk of the British Columbia Supreme Court read these words out loud in Vancouver on October 7, 1919. For more than thirteen years after he was charged with murder, Simon Gunanoot lived ahead of B.C. provincial police, Pinkerton's men and bounty hunters in his ancestral hunting grounds near the headwaters of the Skeena River northeast of Hazelton, northwest of Takla Lake and in bush country as far up as the Yukon border. How far south is not known. Simon could make fifty miles a day in the thickest brush. He gave himself up in 1919, with enough trapping money for a lawyer, and was found not guilty.

But Simon, who would have known best what to do, gave no sign to Rose. The woman wouldn't get into the Fisheries truck, but walked into the woods along the river bank, where she must have waited all day for the night freight to come through while she lay down on the railway crossing.

By the time Rose's bathtub self-portraits with her eyes closed were taken, the sound of ·the waterfront train was still streaming in the window, but the possibility of Simon Gunanoot, outlaw-savior, bearing the means of survival, even in the city, had been abandoned. Instead, Rose was imagining a fleet of small golden fish—maybe some of the velvet black Moors too—swimming in the bath with her.

The tiny motions of their translucent fins, tails and mouths would stir the water and inadvertently, almost absentmindedly, smoothe her sharp points into softness before she gets out of the bath to go to bed.

In the morning, she bought looking-for-work clothes and a Nikon FM with the *Florentina* money. The black skirt and sweater earned part-time work shelving books at the Fraser branch library. The library provided grocery money and glimpses of other roses in the reference section.

Folklore dictionaries revealed that the rose sprang from the first menstrual blood of Psyche, the virgin soul, according to Gnostic scriptures, when she fell in love with Cupid as Eros. The five-fold petalled layers of the rose belonged to many goddesses' mysteries, as well as to witches' pentacles before they became Mary's wreath of roses in the rosary. In Roman times, a rose was Venus' flower, worn as a badge by her sacred prostitutes.

Rose flipped through pages about prostition on her coffee break. *The Vancouver Field Study of Prostitution: Working Papers on Pornography and Prostitution Report No. 8* suggested, after the deduction of projected overhead costs, an income ranging from nothing to around $22,000. Unsurprising findings from field researchers: Working without a pimp, the more you do beyond a blow job or a straight lay, the more you make.

The Dictionary of Saints offered:

Rose of Lima, recluse, B. at Lima. 1586; d. there, 1617; cd

1671; f.d. 30 August. Isabel Flores y del Olivia, known as Rose, was the first person in the Americas to be canonized as a saint; she was the daughter of Spanish parents in Peru. They were in straitened circumstances, and Rose worked hard to help them by growing flowers and doing embroidery and other needlework. She firmly declined to consider marriage; from the age of twenty she was a Dominican tertiary, and lived in a summer house in the garden of her home. Here she passed long hours in prayer; her retiringness and the cruelty of the penances she inflicted upon herself provoked the criticism of her family and friends, and her mystical experiences and the temptations she suffered became the subject of an ecclesiastical inquiry. St. Rose bore her adversities with uncomplaining patience, and her sympathy with the suffering of others found an outlet in care for the sick, the poor, Indians and slaves; she is looked on today as the originator of social services in Peru.

She finished her namesake research with the library's newest garden book and its revelation of Explorer roses bred in Canada: Alexander MacKenzie, Henry Hudson, John Cabot, and others, including Simon Fraser, an indefatigable bright pink.

Idling along the fiction shelves with her book cart, Rose bypassed Margaret Atwood, Alice Munro and Margaret Laurence, thinking them dangerously likely to have written novels containing some restless Canadian women, minor characters who disappointed people. Instead, she consulted Anna Karenina, Jane Eyre, Lara Guishar, Becky Thatcher and Madame Bovary in search of lightning-fast solutions for a woman whose money was melting as she sickened of the library, the land and herself.

The English Bay apartment girls from ten years ago had turned into lawyers with engagement rings, and a high-school French teacher. They served Rose vegetarian and Thai dinners on condominium balconies, and asked her what she was going to do now she was finished with adventures. She never answered.

Now, on the beach where the afternoon tide has dropped well below *The Woman Who Fell From Heaven*, Rose can admit that, after more than a year in the city down south all that time ago, she was happy to discard advice from women saints, literary heroines and friends in favour of the words of Herman Melville and a man called Ishmael:

Whenever I find myself growing grim about the mouth; whenever it is a damp, drizzly November in my soul; whenever I find myself involuntarily pausing before coffin warehouses, and bringing up the rear of every funeral I meet; ...then I account it high time to get to sea as soon as I can.

At Sea

*T*wo thousand Polish deepsea fishermen know the waters off the west coast of Vancouver Island as well as they know the Baltic Sea. Poland's Pacific fleet works offshore on voyages of five months or more, fishing pollock on the Bering Sea, then moving to the hake grounds within Canada's two hundred sea mile limit on the Pacific coast from June to November. Vancouver is home port for the ships, but their crews arrive from Poland twice a year. In Canadian waters, each foreign vessel carries a Fisheries observer who monitors all fishing and processing operations to provide a presence to the foreign fleet: emphasizing Canadian sovereignty in the two hundred-mile zone.

"This is...*Antares, Indus, Rekin, Parma, Wlojnik, Marlin, Delfin, Arcturus, Mors, Gemini, Kantar, Otol, Acamar, Cassiopeia.* Call sign Sierra Quebec India Juliet...call sign Uniform Sierra Oscar Tango...."

After the first time, when Rose boards a Polish ship at sea, she knows how it will be. She'll jump from the deck of the tug or the Canadian dragger at the top of a swell, grab the rope ladder dangling over the side of the ship like a line trailing from the roof of a skyscraper, and climb. The deck bo's'n and the fishermen will be waiting for her at the top. They'll grab her arms and haul her onto the boat deck. She'll smile tentatively. They'll smile back out of bearded, hard-mouthed faces, relieved that she already knows her way to the bridge.

On the bridge, the captain will shake her hand and send for the chief steward to show her to a cabin. There will be eighty or more men on board, and on this first day together, Rose and the crew will begin to make a bargain between them. She will not mention the cockroaches in her cabin, or her bunk, separated from the noise of the main winch only by a thin bulkhead, or her cabin door, which opens into the wind on an outside deck. Neither the captain nor the technolog (the factory manager) will blame Rose for the Canadian Fisheries regulations on the prohibition of salmon, halibut and herring, or the two-percent rockfish quota. The fishermen on deck will sharpen her sampling knife, give her a thick blue seamen's sweater like theirs and share their coffee rations. Below decks in the factory, Rose will hand out cinnamon gum, and help kick dogfish out the scuppers when the Baader filleting machines break down and when hake back up on the conveyor line. The men will forgive her when she shrieks at them because they haven't set aside the ling cod for her to weigh and record.

Her name will become Joanna or Joasha, but the captain will always be "Captain," even to the chief engineer and the radio officer, who have known him since they were boys together in the maritime school in Gdansk after the war.

When the ship hasn't received enough fish from the Canadian joint venture trawlers by midnight, and must set and haul with her own gear further out to sea through the night, she'll stand beside the captain in the chartroom as his ship moves through the dark. He might trace an imaginary course, through the Inside Passage, across Milbanke Sound, perhaps up Dean Channel to Bella Coola, or across Hecate Strait to the Queen Charlottes, coastal voyages this ship will never make. On some ships, the Polish captain may ask about the Haida or Captain Cook or the meaning of river and inlet names up the coast, knowing that his foreign woman Fisheries observer will tell him stories then, until the ship reaches her new position.

Offshore, Rose is safe from the land and its questions. Sea time for Fisheries observers on foreign ships is usually at least forty days, sometimes sixty, sometimes more. Number of women on board a Polish fishing ship at sea: one. But the work fills the empty field in the country of her mind. Work is: measuring cod ends full of twenty or thirty tonnes of hake; wading knee-deep in the fish on deck to grab a ling cod or yelloweye rockfish to measure and record as bycatch; making diagrams of the below-decks factory and fish meal plant; monitoring fish processing and testing the efficiency of filleting and head-gutting machines in order to check the amount of frozen product produced against the deck estimate; charting the ship's position night and day, and checking the vessel's logs; watching for offal being dumped instead of turned into fish meal; counting all cargo offloaded to mother ship carriers; sexing, weighing, measuring and recording the stomach contents of one hundred and fifty kilograms of hake each time the ship moves into a new sampling area; otolith sampling hake and sometimes rockfish. Otolith aging structure sampling means gathering three baskets of randomly chosen fish:

Grasp the fish firmly in the left hand. Cut down behind the eyes, then back across the head. Lift the flesh using tweezers or the point of a knife to remove from the jellied brain cavity two tiny ear stones that look like fringed white feathers curved into shallow boat-shaped bones. The ridges of these otolith bones can be read to reveal the age of the fish. Wipe the otoliths clean. Place them in the numbered sampling tray. Record fish length, sex and catch location.

The sea out of sight of land makes a moat around Rose. The cascade of incomprehensible Polish speech makes another defence until she learns to understand one word in ten. But in the sea time, she knows the hard-mouthed men on the deck crews as well as she knows anyone.

Rose one night, three or four years into the observer job, is on board the Polish trawling ship *Antares*, national fishing with the vessel's own cod end and gear about forty sea miles offshore. She's part of a scene more real to her by now than nail polish and film purchases, hair brushing before Arbutus Street, bank account reckonings or any other transactions that take place in the hurried, brittle shore time between voyages.

She's crowded together with the deck crew on the

bench in the passageway, waiting to haul. The bo's'n's beard stirs on his chest when the wind flails past the door to the deck. Kryztof, who looks like a patient Byzantine Christ when his shoulders bow under the weight of the warp cable, snores lightly now. Splicing knives dangle in the hands of Andrzej and Andrzej, leaning on each other next to Rose. They're dark-haired boys who grin even when the line lets out that dry, warning squeal and one of them has to step out on deck to signal the bridge to stop hauling. On her other side is the "gangsterski", with dolphins and mermaids dancing up his arms into the rolled sleeves of his grey sweater.

Swells rock Rose and the Polish fishermen, shoulder to shoulder, in time with the sway of blue-checked shirts and spare gloves drying on the pipes overhead. Half-drunk tea in glasses wedged between their booted feet tilts from port to starboard. When the captain's voice crackles out of the intercom, they're up at once, but Marek, the "gangsterski," has to hold Rose's arm until she's steady. The bo's'n hands him her hard hat, and with infinite gentleness, he sets it on her head. Kryztof turns up her collar, the bo's'n nods and the six of them step into the wall of wind on deck.

She's more of a stranger on board Canadian boats commanded to take a Fisheries observer. More than once, it's necessary to offer Richard's name as a reference. And Richard himself, delivering live cod in Ucluelet while Rose is packing her gear down to an unlikely looking craft for a black cod trip into international waters beyond the two hundred-sea mile limit, only says, "Rose, you got more guts than I do."

Black cod trips usually begin in Port Hardy at the top end of Vancouver Island. Day one on the *Anne Sonora* and the crew's still in shock from having to take a woman Fisheries observer with them. Southeast wind in Goletas Channel and Rose's teeth are clenched against the land with its cedar and salal signalling the limit of the sea's reach. Nothing belonging to the warm-blooded earth can help her now. The camera and the blue silk crepe dress aren't out here at Nahwitti Bar. Only *Anne Sonora*'s forever heeling wooden hull is between Rose and the sea.

One of the deckhands asks the others, "Does she know we're not coming in until we're full?"

Thirty-two hours northwest of Nahwitti Bar is Bowie Seamount, black cod country, twelve hundred fathoms deep, almost two hundred miles offshore just inside Canada's western sea limit.

"Bowie Seamount isn't the end of the world," the engineer says, "but you can see the end of the world from here."

When *Anne*'s engines are idling on the open sea at last, the captain mumbles about spending so goddamn much time on Bowie, he needs a post office box labelled 53 degrees 18' N, 135 degrees W.

A horizon dissolving into water surrounds what's left of the world like the rim of an overturned bowl. Albatrosses follow the boat. *Anne Sonora* mutters and sighs. No land, no other boat or ship or plane or any other distraction from emptiness is in sight. Not that Rose needs to be saved from drowning, but it's necessary to give thanks for the homely matters *Anne* mixes among her hoists, gears and chains. Gratitude is due to: scabbed white paint on the wood of the cabin against Rose's back; to the round solidity of the deckrail under her hands; to the slight lean on the galley door frame; to the shelf above the table caging ketchup, mustard, salt, pepper, hot sauce, Cheeze Whiz, two kinds of jam and a huge jar of peanut butter; and to her place on the bench beside the deckhands at meal times.

The galley is *Anne Sonora*'s clean, well-lighted place. To cut down on fish blood and scales in here, the cook decrees no one is allowed to wear raingear above their knees at the table. This means Rose and the deckhands roll down their Helly Hansen pants and enter the galley walking like large, awkward babies with slipped diapers.

Anne's galley is a sanctuary in which seawater sometimes washes the floor. The cook says, "Don't need to listen to marine weather reports on this boat. We got wind, wave and swell height right here in the galley since she shifted her whole fucking cabin coming across the Sound in a blow last winter." But more than storm damage makes its presence felt in the galley.

"Stove's a goddamn foundry," the engineer tells Rose. "Came out of the penitentiary. Probably they sentenced prisoners to cook on it. Or be baked in it. Stove's probably as old as *Anne* herself." His voice floats up from the engine department, "One of the pumps down here is marked 1943. But the main engine's Caterpillar and the starboard auxilliary's a Cummins, so they'll both be turning over even after...."

The *Anne Sonora* was built at a shipyard in San Diego before Rose was born. Stem: Raked. Stern: Fantail. Build: Caravel. The first time she steps into *Anne*'s wheelhouse, she's in Grade One at Maple Ridge School on Cypress Street again, thirty years ago. The smell of wet hardwood and wool sweaters and the pounding of her heart are the same.

"The old girl still turns a dollar, if we shove her," the captain says between mouthfuls of sausage and eggs. "She paid for herself on tuna in the Gulf of Mexico, then halibut in the Bering Sea. Guy who owns her now took out her main mast to get more traps on deck so she can do it again on black cod. Course he don't come out here and roll around with her."

Losing the heavy mast causes *Anne* to roll without ceasing. She breathes hard, rising slowly from a deep port side stagger, pauses, trembling, falls to starboard, but always returns, rides upright for an instant, then continues pitching from side to side. Only one of the men speaks against her for this.

"Roll slut, roll!" are the words he grinds out when he staggers on deck, the way they all do.

For thirty days on the *Anne Sonora* offshore at Bowie Seamount, there are black cod, strong streamlined bodies to be clubbed, scraped clean, and frozen. Sweet, firm flesh worth $6.32 a pound in Japan.

The men clip wire-mesh traps, baited with frozen fish scraps, onto a mile of line unreeling from the stern drum.

The strings of traps are fastened to numbered floats flying black commercial flags, then left to soak sixteen, eighteen, twenty hours in the darkness twelve hundred fathoms down. The fish feeding in the deepest levels in Bowie's shadowed canyons are blind. Strings were left soaking while *Anne* and her crew ran to Port Hardy and back, so there is work from the first morning on the seamount and forever after.

The captain asks the men on deck if they've noticed a black cod trap is heavier than a racing form, and if they just now woke up and figured out they're not still back in town.

To Rose, crouching on deck with her sampling gear and a Rite-in-the-Rain notebook, he says, "The other guy who runs this scow when I'm in town, he'll just tell the crew, 'Plenty of good men left on shore' if they complain about anything out here. Bitch any more and he'll hand out a Norwegian wheel turn, six hours on and stay on."

He orders the cook, "No fuckin' dinner until the fuckin' fish are in the fuckin' freezer if it takes all night." This means roast beef, mashed potatoes, gravy, asparagus, corn, white buns, green salad and fruit salad at 0200 after the first day of fishing.

After two weeks of eighteen hour days, Rose stands on the deck with the crew, waiting for strings of black cod traps to surface, uncertain if this is morning or evening. Light stays on the edge of the sky all night out here in early summer. Ten strings are soaking. Fifty-five traps to a string. She shifts her weight from side to side on the sliding deck, staring down into the water or up into the sky. "Sister

Anne, Sister Anne," she wants to call across the plain of the sea like Bluebeard's wife, "Is there anyone coming?" but *Anne Sonora* and the men are all there is.

"You only done half your hard time on here, girl," one of the deckhands says. "You heard about this guy who escapes from jail? He's on the run, stows away on a black cod boat, then when they go in to deliver, he runs up the dock fast as he can go, yelling for the cops and gives himself up. Begs to get off the black cod boat and go back to jail."

Talking about black cod boats and docks reminds the cook of another story. "Different boat, outside Gowgaia in a bad sea. The old man and his two boys are up in the wheelhouse with their survival suits on, screaming at us to shift the traps on deck, get some balance back on her. We're slanted over pretty bad. This young kid, first trip, he starts crying, 'We're going to die, we're going to die!' I had to hit him. 'Snap out of it,' I scream myself. 'Help me move this fuckin' gear so maybe we won't die.' So we get the traps shifted and get into Gowgaia Bay, God knows how. I see that kid sometimes when we deliver in Port Hardy. He's happy driving the ore truck for Utah Mines. Won't even come onto the dock. Me, I'm still waiting for my number to come up out here."

"Shut the fuck up," someone says.

The traps wheel out of the sea festooned with pink and white coral branches and lava fragments. At dawn on the twenty-second day, a green glass float, almost submerged by its underwater load of barnacles, drifts alongside the string of traps. The engineer and the deckhand who curses the *Anne Sonora*'s constant rolling are the ones who get it onboard and give it to Rose.

There is always the weather.

Marine Forecast, Offshore Bowie, Northern Section. Winds southeasterly forty to gales forty-five knots, shifting to easterly forty overnight. Periods of rain. Seas four to five metres. Outlook: winds rising again to gale force southeast.

There is always the rolling. Fish hatches almost full, heavy with ballast, *Anne* still rolls. The diesel in the tanks, the coffee in cups lifted to the mouths of Rose and the men, the thin jelly in their brain pans and the blood running on the decks and in their bodies slide from port to starboard, then fore and aft. The captain, the engineer, the cook, the deckhands and Rose are joined to the boat in restless, liquid motion.

After twenty-eight days, there are dreams. Rose is walking on grassy paths in Regina. The engineer is underneath *Anne*, looking at her zincs. Dreams lead to ghosts and Scarlett Point where the grass is all bright and green and looks like its been mowed. Haunted ground, according to the cook. He heard it from some Japanese fishermen. Ghosts lead to albatrosses. The engineer believes they are the spirits of drowned halibut fishermen. But the cook reports he saw this guy come out of his wheelhouse to shoot an albatross two seasons back . He pikes it out of the water, plucks it, sticks it in the oven, eats one bite and chucks it overboard.

By now, the captain talks mostly on the radio. "*Snow*

Pass, Anne Sonora, Snow Pass, Anne Sonora, Viking Warrior, Viking Warrior, Anne Sonora, Anne Sonora out." Then to himself, "I can hear them boats talking like they were down in the galley and they're how many hundred miles south, but can they pick me up? Do they answer? Probably forgot we're out here."

Rose thinks the land itself has probably forgotten them. But by the time they've steamed fifty hours south to the Fraser, the open ocean is present only in the lag time between their eyes, devouring factories and apartments on the riverbanks, and their still-slow, intermittent speech. Their feet cling to the deck of the *Anne Sonora*, settled low now in fresh water. She's so heavy with dollars and fish, and moves so slowly in the river traffic, she's almost stable at last. Car drivers on the Knight Street Bridge regard her briefly, not curious, as she backs awkwardly into the North Sea unloading dock. Once the boat is tethered to the cleats on the pilings, the men are impatient to be done with her.

Rose is a while getting off and a week remembering to find the old man who used to own the *Anne Sonora* when she still had her mast.

What he tells her is, "I loved my first boat, but not her. Not *Anne*. Everything I had was paid for, including my wife, until I went out and got the *Anne Sonora*. Her fuel tanks were in the bow, so she ploughed the water, and that slanted stern made her a pig in a following sea. You say they took her mast off? She'd have rolled like a whore."

For years, the long rolling climb and fall of offshore swells stilled restlessness in Rose. The deep ocean has no eddies or local currents. These disturbances are made by shards of land intruding into the sea's motion. Where there is no land, there is swelling sea. No matter how fair the weather, the ocean offshore never quietens the way it can when sheltered by the land. The rocking, rolling sweep of water builds slowly, making broad swells on the sweetest days, higher and sharper hills when wind rises, taking days to die down after a storm. Or a ground swell rises on some mid-ocean storm a thousand sea miles away, and finds you at last, no matter the wind where you are. The wide, slow seduction of an offshore swell reaches up into Rose's body and thoughts the way the ceaseless tilting and rocking penetrates everyone who can bear it out there.

You dream more at sea. Everyone does, moving in a forgotten, familiar-again liquid world. Day and night dreams. Rose daydreams the smell of hot dust hanging in the air at Meziadin Junction on the Nass River while she's standing at the stern of foreign ships hauling thirty tonnes of hake. At night, she dreams she has a child, or is a child, or a dolphin. Captains dream of wheat or rye fields rippling like the sea, or of steering their vessels through narrow paved passageways requiring fearful manoeuvring in Gdansk or Warsaw or Maple Ridge shopping malls.

The rising, falling, side-to-side sliding power of the sea streams up a two-legged body to its fork and on through the belly, slows to keep time with the bone-caged heart before tilting the brain's fluid jelly, then pounding on in a ceaseless circle of motion. Blood thunders new the first few days of deep-sea voyages, beats pleasingly against starched sheets and rough wool blankets on a narrow bunk moving sweetly, strongly beneath you. The up and down of the sea is inside Rose now, entering, enticing, swallowing. She's coming home, giving in to the fluid force that was the necessary beginning, and will be the end.

When the weather conditions become dangerous, there is only one possibility open to a sailing ship: escape. Fleeing from the storm permits a ship and crew to reach safety, and perhaps also to discover new lands, far from the supposedly safe routes of the liners and merchant ships. You know the name of this sailing ship; she's called Desire.

-Henry LaBorit, *Praise to Escape*

Desire for union with a substance other than your own, can be indistinguishable from the need for dissolution. When the *Anne Sonora* sank in late winter twilight off the west coast of the Charlottes, Rose was between boats, sitting by the window in the Scarlet Ibis pub at Holberg on the logging road to the west coast of Vancouver Island, trying to decide if she had enough heart to hike into San Josef Bay, or enough wine for the man at the pool table who turned to her after every shot, or only enough of anything for the prayer every true pirate, fisherman and sailor makes on land whether he knows the words or not: Dear Cypris, If thou savest those at sea, I perish, wrecked, ashore. Save also me. Cypris being Aphrodite, the sea-born, of Cyprus.

Anne went down slowly, allowing her crew to step dry-footed into her liferaft. The galley lights, and the deck light called day, switched on when the alarm sounded, gleamed underwater for long minutes, sinking so reluctantly into the dark that the trawler coming to rescue the crew in the life raft scarcely needed a searchlight.

Russian ships work in Canada's western offshore waters too. Because Rose allows the Russians to know she's often absent from them, and their ship, and any meaning she might find in herself, as well as being a woman who works and laughs and weeps with them for months on end at sea, she's sure they would recognize the welcoming grace granted by *Anne*'s underwater lights. They would understand too, without words, why a logger would need to turn an old bunkhouse in the rain forest into an English-style pub, and why his wife, Ruby, would name it after a flower from her first home in Jamaica.

Because the Russians allow her to know them as they do her, the story they tell about the man who used to be second officer on the *Aleksei Chirikov* joins her to him. Because all Russians sail away again into other, unreachable lives, it's safe enough to look into and love every tough, bewildered-by-perestroika man and woman—always three other women: the bufetchitsa (the officers' steward), a doctor, and a laundry woman—on board each Russian ship. Because the Russians on the *Aleksei Chirikov* gave Rose the second officer's cabin when she boarded the ship at Constance Bank anchorage outside Victoria Harbour, she can imagine how it was for him before she ever lay down in his bunk, or hung her work clothes in his tin locker.

The second officer and his shipmates were not the first

Russians to sail for North American coastal waters from Kamchatka.

1. In Kamchatka or some other place build one or two boats with decks.

2. On these boats sail near the land which goes to the north which (since no one knows where it ends) it seems is part of America.

3. Discover where it is joined to America, and go as far as some town belonging to a European power; if you encounter some European ship, ascertain from it what is the name of the nearest coast, and write it down and go ashore personally and obtain firsthand information, locate it on a map and return here.

-Instructions from Empress Ekaterina Alekseeva to Captain Vitus Bering, Februrary 25, 1725

Aleksei Chirikov was a twenty-two year old lieutenant under Captain Vitus Bering on the first Kamchatka expedition to search for the land or the strait between Siberia and America in 1728.

On June 4, 1741, Chirikov sailed from Avacha Bay on the Siberian coast as captain on the Sv. Pavel, accompanying Bering's vessel, Sv. Petr, on the second Kamchatka expedition.

The two vessels lost sight of each other in a storm two weeks later. Bering reached the mouth of the Copper River in Alaska, and the group of islands off the Alaska peninsula, naming the Shumagin Islands to honour the first death from scurvy in his crew. When scurvy affected more crew members, including Bering himself, the Sv. Petr turned back to Siberia, but was wrecked on one of the Komandorskie Islands in a November storm.

Vitus Bering and more than forty of his men survived the shipwreck. After ensuring plans to build a new vessel from the remains of Sv. Petr, Bering died on the island later named for him. Forty-six men on his crew eventually reached Avacha Bay in the vessel they had built, nine months later on August 26, 1742.

Aleksei Chirikov had searched diligently for the Sv.Petr two days in late June of 1741, the length of time Bering had strictly ordered, and had then continued his own voyage, sighting northern California, then exploring and mapping the Alaskan coast and the Aleutian Islands. Some of his men did not return from shore expeditions. Others, including his lieutenants, died of scurvy. Chirikov himself was too weak to go on deck for most of the return voyage.

The navigator, Ivan Elagin, was in command of the ship from September 21, 1741. Chirikov recorded in his report to the Russian Admiralty: "I gave him as much assistance as I could (since thanks to God's mercy I was of sound mind), and by studying the calculations of our voyage from the journal, I advised him what course to follow....On October 8 at 0700, with God's mercy, we sighted the land of Kamchatka, and on the 10th at 0900 we entered Avacha Bay and lay at anchor. By then we had consumed all the fresh water we had except for two barrels distilled from seawater by boiling it in kettles....With God's help we reached the present bay of Petropavlovsk on October 12. The harbour in Avacha Bay became the city of Petropavlovsk, the city of Saints Petr and Pavel, Peter and Paul.

The second officer had drifted safely past more than half of the *Aleksei Chirikov*'s winter fishing voyage on the Bering and Okhotsk seas before he enmeshed himself in a net of memory and dreams. Days, he'd worked his bridge watches along with a shift in the processing factory below decks when the catch was heavy. Nights, he drank tea with the third officer, or sat in the mess room to watch 16 mm films in which soldiers or gypsies or Cossacks streamed across an empty plain, their silhouettes dark against the sky as they sang a sombre, defiant chorus into the distance. He had kept up his paperwork. He had slept.

In his bunk, wool blankets weighted the length of his body, filling his nose and mouth with their cold animal odour. A white cotton pillowcase transmitted the slight dampness of its enclosed feathers to his cheek until he turned and crossed his arms over his chest to lie, unmoving in the first shallow layer of sleep. Later, he would curve himself onto his right side, always the starboard side to steer away from nightmares at sea.

He allowed only itinerant, easily ignored characters to cross the geography of his dreams during the first half of the voyage: the eight-year-old boy he used to be in the high-ceilinged flat in the south; Konstantin from next door at the same age, shivering in an unravelling sweater, one of his eyes bright with mischief, the other dark with foreboding; the ghost of Vitus Bering, his voice mixed into the snowmelt in the Anadyr River, supposed to be telling him how to get upstream to the source, but he's speaking some unintelligible foreign tongue only explorers understand.

After nearly three months at sea, the second officer weakened and let down the barrier at the border of his dreams, exhausted, perhaps by the stubborn southeast gale that had shunted the ship around the Shelikhova Gulf for days. Asleep on the long swell the winds had left behind, he saw himself, not the solemn-faced child of earlier nights, but the same man he was on the ship, standing again in a room full of spilled wine and shouting in the port of Petropavlovsk. A woman leaned over, whispering words he couldn't hear in the dream, any more than he'd heard them when he sat across from her, cinnamon-and-sweat-scented, in the flesh the night before the Aleksei Chirikov sailed.

The second officer opened his eyes and wedged the bulk of his top blanket behind his back to hold his body still as the ship rolled down one side, hesitated, returned upright for an instant, then rolled again. Pushing his feet against the bottom of the bunk to stretch the cramps that knotted his legs almost every night at sea, he wondered why he'd wanted to escape the woman in the bar when he had nothing to do, once he was standing in the muddy street outside the place, but lurch toward the pier where the *Aleksei Chirikov* lay waiting for him. He didn't understand how he had been able to recreate the Petropavlovsk woman from memory so easily, even if she was only a dream, when most mornings as he rose and braced himself against the tin locker to keep his balance, for the first moment or two, he couldn't remember the *Aleksei Chirikov*'s name, or call sign, or even which ocean they were fishing.

The tin locker's shabby, unchanging presence was a

comfort to him, as well as a reminder of where he was. Over the course of the voyage, he had come to know his cabin better than he'd ever known the rooms he shared with his wife when he was still married. Those rooms had sometimes seemed as if they should belong to another man, someone whose fingers didn't catch on the web of his wife's crocheted shawl, tearing the strands and making her cry; a man who smiled more, who knew without being told that when he returned from the ship, his wife wanted him to dance with her beside their bed before they got into it.

The cabin's furnishings had become members of the second officer's family, whether they were new and unspoiled, like the small mirror that Sasha, the deck bo's'n, had supplied, or worn with use, as was the tin locker, whose gaping door required constant contrivance with tape and cord to keep it from banging relentlessly. There was a hook that reminded him, he couldn't say why, of one of his girl cousins each time it loosened itself on a fifteen-degree port roll to chime a pure belled note against the steel door frame. His armchair required him to lean to the right and slightly forward to accommodate his body to its crooked frame. When he had finished his bridge watch each day, he sat in this chair at the plywood table bolted to the bulkhead. The table and shelf above it held icons of the unimaginably distant earth, remembrances of vanished kitchens and garden plots, things the second officer always intended to eat or drink or admire, but more often forgot until they rotted or spilled or rolled off the table: soft, pink-cheeked apples and hard-boiled eggs with grey, finger-smudged shells, given to him by Raisa, the ship's bufetchitsa; hard toffees and lemon drops wrapped in purple and white paper printed with dancing horses which always stuck to the candy; a packet of black tea leaning against a glassful of coarse-grained sugar crystals; a cracked, flowered cup; a bundle of birch twigs, the jagged-edged leaves gone brittle and dull, but still green.

The plywood table was intended for the paperwork required by the second officer's additional duties as provisions officer and assistant supercargo. If the pale northern sun pushed through the morning sky, he might see the shadow of a petrel or some other seabird fly across his papers before he went up to the bridge. A ribbon of light refracted from the waves below could dance over the cargo logs and up the bulkhead. He worked at the table when he had finished his watch on the bridge and was not needed in the factory below decks during the late afternoon and on into the evening, comforted by the yellow gleam of his desk light in the early dark as he sorted food lists and cargo hold plans and tallied cartons filled with frozen headed and gutted or filleted pollock.

He stopped writing now and then to stare through the salt-smeared glass at the darkening sea beside him, then glance at the picture pinned above his table. This picture, torn from an old issue of *Novy Mir*, showed a dusty white road, a path, really, winding through green countryside. The curves of the road were entirely human and full of promise, he thought each time he looked at them, in a way the sea never was. Life is not a walk across a field.

In the fourth month of the voyage, the second officer looked up at the white road picture, and remembered his father's mother reciting the field proverb at every calamity from a cracked egg to the death of her daughter-in-law. The old woman had slept on a couch with him when he was small and his mother was still alive, when they lived in the Crimea. His grandmother sighed often in her sleep, terrifying him with her muttering about famine bread, the dense, bitter loaves made from grass she'd eaten when the grain was gone, years before he was born. She woke him once in the middle of the night, he remembered, to tell him she had dreamed she saw Lev Tolstoi on the boardwalk in Sevastopol. She was afraid of him, she said. He looked angry and as if he had no legs. It had all truly happened, she insisted, once upon a time when she was a girl, on the boardwalk in Sevastopol by the Black Sea.

Tolstoi must have been sitting in a wheeled wicker-basket chair, the second officer thought when he awoke before dawn the next morning, if it had been him at all. He cared nothing for Tolstoi. Chekhov, maybe. There was some value to him. He had visited the ports and prisons on Sakhalin, for one thing, and, according to his wife, he had uttered an incomprehensible question about sailors as he lay dying. The second officer felt he would have been able to tell Anton Chekhov what he wanted to know about sailors if he'd been at his bedside.

"I know my work," he thought. "I know the Bering Sea and the Barents, the north Pacific and the Okhotsk Sea. Awake and asleep, I remember the land, even if I no longer know what to do with it, or it with me, when I'm on shore. That's all there is to being a sailor."

Weariness washed over the second officer. He smoothed the bedclothes and lay back in his bunk, but sleep was gone from him. He opened his eyes and saw the shapes of the armchair and the tin locker, huge and strange in the dark. He got up to unlatch his porthole, put out his hand to feel the river of wind and rain flowing past the Aleksei Chirikov. He touched his cool, wet palm to his cheek and his tiredness retreated a little. There was a street in Moscow called Sailors' Rest, he had heard, although he had never been able to find it on his hurried visits to the city. Now, standing beside the porthole open to the night, he wondered if Sailors' Rest was well-lighted or dark, if people walked along it cheerfully crowded together, calling out to one another and smiling at known faces, or if they went alone, their shoulders hunched over bags and bundles, their eyes avoiding one another's glances.

These imagined scenes slid away from the second officer, and in their place came a memory of a foreign street where he had stood, suspended in the night for a moment, on his way back to the ship. He couldn't remember which ship. Not the *Aleksei Chirikov*. The side of the street he had walked along lay on the edge of a small park, facing a line of stores whose clouded front windows were shuttered with cardboard for the night. A man's running shoe, blue and white, thick-soled, lay on its side, close to his feet when he stopped. Its mate waited on the grass beside the pavement. He heard the soft, repeated thud of a basketball bouncing from backboard to concrete within the park, although the player was hidden by the complicated and delicate structure of wooden bleachers.

He recalled the huge, broad-leafed maple trees glowing copper under the street lights beside the park, and how he had, for that moment, seemed to be in the right place at the right time on land, sheltering beneath the trees in the green, warm darkness in a port he no longer remembered. Not Dutch Harbour. Not Bergen. Maybe St. John's. Maybe Vancouver. Niechivo. It didn't matter, he decided.

His watch time was nearly upon him although there was still no light in the sky. He washed and dressed in the dark, closed the porthole and latched his door to the bulkhead so anyone might see he was not in his cabin. He walked up to the bridge and nodded to Viktor, who'd worked as his helmsman through four voyages. He fixed the *Aleksei Chirikov*'s position on the chart and marked it in the log, then looked at the radar screen, which was cluttered with rain, but gave no cause for alarm. The nearest vessel, a grain ship, was more than fifteen miles away. The closest land, Cape Lopatka at the end of the Kamchatka Península, lay four days' running time to the northeast.

The second officer smiled at Viktor, touched his shoulder lightly, and went out onto the port deck in the rain. The bridge door swung back and forth behind him, allowing Viktor to see him as he climbed the deck rail and balanced for an instant on its slick rounded surface before he stepped off into the dark air and water.

The new second officer on *Aleksei Chirikov*'s May voyage

was put into the double cabin with the third officer. Except for the motormen, the chief cook and the helmsman, everyone on board had gathered on the boat deck and the wings of the bridge when the ship neared the latitude and longitude where the second officer had gone over the side. They had long since forgiven him for their lost fishing time and for the hours of useless searching through black water. Sasha, the deck bo's'n, still had the second officer's silver penknife, the tiny one from Odessa with flowers and leaves engraved on the handle. He had meant to return the knife the very day the man had drowned himself. Anna from the laundry had found a dark hair clinging to the pillowcase when she stripped the bedclothes from the second officer's bunk. She had shed a few secret tears, then confided them to Raisa Sergeyeva, still the ship's bufetchitsa, who told the pillowcase tale to others on board. One of the fishermen from the trawl deck was thinking of writing a song to commemorate the death of the second officer.

Despite these proofs of luxurious and satisfying grief, neither Rose now nor anyone else on the *Aleksei Chirikov* felt the second officer's suicide was mad, or even unreasonable. Those who stayed on shore might not know it, they thought, but the more remarkable situation on this, the last, or any other voyage was that no others of the ship's company had decided yet to end the tension that rises in those who cling to an eggshell craft, knowing how smoothly the land rolls on without them, while determinedly keeping separate from the sea who cradles us and pushes us away and reaches out, sucking and roaring and yearning after us.

The second officer's maple trees glowing copper under the street lights were in Oppenheimer Park on Powell Street in Vancouver, along Rose's route to the ships at Ballantyne Pier. It would be wise of her to make the ship after the *Aleksei Chirikov* her last. She may be able to give up going to work as a Fisheries observer on foreign ships if she can think what to do with her work clothes.

The black wool sweater warming Rose late on an October afternoon on Roberson Point is last of her work clothes. This sweater, much travelled on land by now, is still enough to bring back one day, an ordinary day, on the last fishing ship.

At 0800, the Polish deep sea trawler Parma *is drifting on a quiet sea at 48 degrees 27' N, 125 degrees 28'W in Canadian Offshore Fishery Zone 5. The blue mountains between Carmanah and Bonilla Point are thirty sea miles off the starboard bow. This morning, Rose wears a hooded green sweatshirt given to her by one of the deck hands on the black cod boat* Anne Sonora. *The green sweatshirt from the* Anne Sonora *is permanently stained with fish blood and smeared with grease from* Parma's *stern winch now, but Rose can't let go of it yet.*

The trawl winches are hauling a cod end on board, so she'll go out on deck in a minute, wearing the gumboots Richard gave her. The boots had appeared brand new on his deck, he told Rose, too small for anyone else. They must have been meant for her, he said. Alert Bay cod fishermen gave her Fred Stanley's red-and-black checkered flannel shirt too, when she first started working at sea with the Poles and the Russians. They knew she was afraid of the foreign ships then, and they thought Fred's sense of humour, as well as his infinite knowledge of fish, might be transmitted to her through his shirt. Besides, they said, Fred Stanley collected flannel shirts, all identical, and he'd never miss this one. The shirt protected Rose through the first offshore voyages on Polish ships, then she gave it to Nikolai Sergeyevich, the trawl bo's'n who needed its comfort even more than she did on the Soviet trawler Aleksei Chirikov. Fred Stanley's shirt is probably still fishing on the Okhotsk Sea, two thousand miles away. On Parma, her shirts are the same blue-and-green cotton worn by every man on the ship except the officers.

In the years when Rose was more at home on the sea than the land, she needed to wear the same shabby Bering Sea coat liners and patched blue jackets the Russians wore, the same wool sweaters and yellow rain gear the Poles used. Some days, standing for hours in the factory below decks measuring hake stomachs or testing the filleting machines, she wore pearls with these clothes.

At 1500, if there are no troubles on the Parma, she lies down, still dressed, to float in shallow sleep on a white-railed bunk in the hospital cabin on the passageway off the starboard side of the trawl deck.

Afternoon dream: she stands at a bus stop on Granville in Vancouver, wearing work clothes smelling of fish and blood, staring at the closed door of the Arbutus Street bus. She knows very well the bus is forbidden to her. She shouldn't even be on the street, or in the city, or on land anywhere. This sanction is immutable, causing panic to thicken in her throat until she sees she's carrying

Parma's *brass bell. The real bell hangs from a steel frame on the
ship's bow, and is so heavy only a twenty-five or thirty-degree
roll could cause it to ring, but in Rose's dream it rests easily in
her arms.*

*Deeper layers of sleep and the seagoing nightgown folded
under the pillow are hours away. The white cotton, ankle-length
nightgown, frilled at wrists and collar, satisfactorily contradicts
the ship's hard edges for Rose, and probably for the Russian and
Polish fishermen who've often seen it stuffed into her dirty jeans
on deck in the dark when* Parma *trawls with her own heavy
gear, hauling night and day. The nightgown isn't beautiful or
even white any more, but rust-marked from too many washings
in distilled seawater running through old pipes. Rose is still glad
to see it after the ship's steel and wood and wire all day.*

*Supper's finished by 2000 hours. Tonight Rose wore silver
crescent-moon earrings and ate with the crew in their mess room,
where aluminum knives, forks and spoons are jammed into tin
cans set on long, oilcloth-covered tables. The trawl bo's'n, the deck
crew and Rose sat together on a bench, pretending they were a
family, while Jesus standing on a green hill regarded them with
great gentleness from his picture pinned to the bulkhead above
the coffee grinder. Supper was borscht and meat pies. The moon
earrings swayed with the roll of the ship.*

At 2230, Parma *moves slowly across dark water to take the
last haul of the day. In a minute or two, along with the deck
crew, Rose will reach into the drying room for a black wool
sweater unravelling at the neck. Rose, the extra one, the not-
Russian, not-Polish, not a crew member, but necessary-in-Canadian-
waters one, is still be part of the* Parma. *At dawn tomorrow,*

the ship will be close to her present position, and the day, like the one just gone, will be as fair and calm as anyone on board has ever known in these waters. Parma, who is old and whose crew fear for her in heavy seas, will steam serenely, her bell silent, firmly fastened to its rightful place on the bow.

Before breakfast, Rose will put on the Alert Bay boots and go down to the factory to see how the night's processing has gone. Behind the huge fish tanks in the factory waits the steering gear. Here, a wooden wheel is set alongside a brass curve turning slowly on either side of a centred, broad unmoving arrow in response to the helm and gyrocompass on the bridge, four decks above. The wheel, the arrow and the curve of the steering gear are connected directly to the rudder, so the vessel could, if necessary, be steered from this deep place within her.

After the Sea

*B*ut after the sea, there is no course, only a dry, uneasy stretch of time. If there's no sea and no river, nothing moistens Rose or her stories, or causes either of them to take a fluid, moving form. Clearly, a woman who has abandoned the Skeena River and marriage, and who knows now that observing fisheries from foreign and Canadian decks means she's not much more to the sea than a passenger, deserves no stories. She gets to stand alone, filled with blood-jumping restlessness, in an empty field.

Onto this arid stage reels the memory of a fleet of fourteen- and fifteen-year-old girls, still sweating the clean diluted salt of children, laughing away the pleasurable prickle of their fear because they know they're going where they're wanted, where they'll be forgiven damp crescents under their arms, smeared frosted lipstick and all other foolishness. Once walking home from the Fisheries office at dusk, Rose saw the Pied Piper Pimp who took the girls out to the ships anchored in Prince Rupert Harbour and moored at the super port. He was coming out of the Salvation Army thrift shop on Third Avenue with an armload of dresses, pink and black, with crinolines.

Rose wants to be going out at dusk now, floating lightly on into the night. Night's promissory notes are cancelled by morning. Night rushes past car and bedroom and bar windows, transforming these enclosures into safe places.

The enclosed, between-decks space on a ship is a lazaret, either at the stern or in the forepeak of the vessel, intended for the stowage of provisions and stores on long voyages. The word may also have an archaic meaning as an isolation hospital for sailors with infectious diseases. Lazaret might be a corruption of 'nazaret' from the 15th century St. Maria di Nazaret church hospital for seamen in Venice. Spare web, lines and corks were kept in the lazaret on the Florentina *and other wooden-hulled salmon seiners up the coast. Offshore, the lazaret on the Polish ship* Delfin *contained a net of copper tubing woven into a still by the electrician.*

But when the word 'lazaret' takes Rose unawares in the after-the-sea time, she sees a dark form there in the lazaret, crouched with arms around knees, head bent to fit into a cramped compartment. She's convinced there's a link between 'lazaret' and 'lazar', the old word for leper.

Waking up chilled, after a fresh air nap in her rock bed in Venn Pass, Rose is inclined, even now, to forgive herself easily for all the men after the sea. She'd willingly undertaken the risk, after all, and received suitable punishment. She hadn't disappointed anyone. More the reverse.

Bathed and blessed in the Pacific light, faintly blue even

in winter, Rose absorbs the fact that the falling tide is more than halfway down to low slack, and that she doesn't remember her own words or thoughts from the nights when she filled emptiness with men. She must have spoken sometimes, said, "Yes," and, "I will," and, "More." She must have, at least once, said, "No," or, "Stop," or, "Let me go." She didn't say, "Please." She would have said it in time, though. She must have been thinking tenderly, now and then, about the soft skin behind men's ears, or the small stretched place in back of their balls where a fingertip can imagine a path up into the inward trembling of their bodies. Occasionally, the withdrawal of flesh from her body must have taken place with a measure of reluctance. Some nights, she must have crooned over the silvery tracks of men's scars, and the tattooed snakes, dragons, eagles and arrows serving as reminders of their younger selves. There are no photographs or sketches from this time.

Instead, there is the remembered act of leaving Wall Street for good because home wasn't supposed to matter, even as a place to stow gear. Boxes went into storage. Clothes in green garbage bags were crushed into the car trunk along with the cameras. No fixed address was an easy place to live until Rose fetched up on the other coast with friends of friends in Lawn in Newfoundland. There, she remembered how home used to be.

"Where do you live then?" Mary Kelly asked when Rose was sitting at the table in her house behind Kelly's General Store. Mary's lived in Lawn all her life. Lawn, population of 1015, has survived on the southwestern shore of Placentia

Bay since the late 1700s, and gave safe harbour to Basque cod fishermen before that.

Rose didn't answer right away. Then, "I used to be out on the boats a lot." A minute or two later, "I'm not in one place any more. With friends in Vancouver sometimes. When I'm not travelling." Mary looked at her as if she were a lost soul.

"Rolling stone," Bill Kelly pronounced while he checked on the tea stewing in a huge pot, then poured out with a steady hand for Alphonse, the postmaster, Evelyn from Halifax, Mary and Rose.

Mary hurried past the subject of home, and someone who chose not to have one. "Rolling stones remind me of spirits," she said. "When my aunt was a girl here in Lawn, she was walking back from Jersey Room out the other end of the harbour one night when a little white stone rolled along the road after her, the one right by the spring well. Rolling and rolling by itself that white stone was. She was some scared."

"That was before the lights," Alphonse said. "There were more ghosts then."

In the darkening evening, everyone around the table looked out beyond the pale clapboards of the store at the edge of the garden, as if they might still see the terrible enchanted stone rolling along the road running past the Powerhouse Brook. Rose thought about Pacific ghosts. John Bruce and his crew night-running past the old Kwak-waka'wakw villages, hearing drums and deep-voiced singing, seeing dancers around huge fires. How when they set out in their seine skiff to join the party, they found only darkness on the beach, no dancers, no signs of fire.

The names of the waters on the way to the villages up the British Columbia coast came back to her: Beware Pass, Blackfish Sound, Tribune Channel, Simoom Sound, Laredo Channel, Browning Entrance, Principe Channel. She turned away from the others at the table then in Lawn, Newfoundland.

"I always used to think there was a ghost in the spring well," Evelyn said. Evelyn Slayney is Leo Tarrant's sister, and Leo's a Lawn fisherman working on the west coast now. Rose made a couple of Hecate Strait groundfish observer trips on his dragger, *Pacific Charmer.* He had his cook make a boiled dinner from home at least once every trip no matter how hard it was blowing.

For Leo's Newfoundland boiled dinner, take a large piece of salt beef and soak in cold water overnight. Put the meat into fresh water and boil it with a little salt pork, forty-five minutes or more. Add turnips first, then carrots, cabbage and potatoes and simmer until done.

Evelyn and Mary and Bill began to talk about whether Leo might take young Owen, Mary's sister's boy, onto the crew of the *Charmer* to give him a chance. Alphonse leaned over to ask how good Leo and the other Newfoundland boys were doing fishing out there on that side anyway, but Rose didn't say much to him, thinking more about her last overnight time on the *Florentina.*

John Bruce's crew, the ones who fished with him since

they were boys—lonely for the boat, any boat—since the old man didn't go out any more, went with Richard and Rose to say goodbye to the mainland inlets before they moved up to Prince Rupert. They went through Wakeman Sound, where mountains rise like walls around the water, to anchor for the night near the mouth of the Kakweikan River in Thompson Sound. Nights in the mainland inlets were sharp cold in late fall, but the boat stayed warm, leaking the familiar smells of diesel, damp wood and coffee, a grain or two charring on the dull black surface of the oil stove.

In the evening when the engine was shut down, they could hear the river pouring into salt water, and the *Florentina* became a nursery of night sounds, her own and those common to all old wood-hulled work boats: the soft static beneath the words of the marine weather report on the radio in the wheelhouse; the rattle from the anchor chain falling down the last fathom, then tapping along the hull when the tide changed; the strained high whine of the sink pump; the clatter of dice on the ridge-edged galley table before supper.

When *Florentina* had floated beyond memory's reach, Rose went down to the room in Kelly's basement where she was to sleep. She lay in bed listening to Mary and Bill and their friends upstairs talking about a girl who had tuberculosis when they were all still children, and how Mary's mother used to make apple snow to tempt her delicate appetite. They talked about whose cattle used to graze in the Big Meadow, about the glitter storm out the highway last winter and about swimming in the Crow's Hole up the brook. They remembered Leo Tarrant's brother Walter, a beautiful man, really beautiful, who drowned when the *Sheila Patricia* burned and sank off Green Island, Nova Scotia. Mary said she never liked meeting anyone on the stairs. Any stairs at all. It was a sure sign of disappointment later in the day. Evelyn asked if the partridge berry patch over on Webber's Ridge was as fine as ever. Everyone talked about who had the fastest boat between here and St. Pierre et Miquelon. No one could remember the name of the priest before the one before this one at Holy Name Church of Jesus up the hill.

Downstairs, Rose turned restlessly in her borrowed bed, finding out she'd forgotten nothing about the places that used to be home up the B.C. coast, only that she'd forbidden herself to remember them. The wash of the sea in Lawn Harbour entered the house every time the front door opened on another visitor.

Lawn Harbour stretches into Placentia Bay. Captain James Cook spent a week in these waters while he charted the Newfoundland coast with the schooner *Grenville*. Legend says Cook was so taken with the incandescent green of the meadows and mosses here against the grey Atlantic that he called the place Lawn. On that summer night in Newfoundland, this was enough evidence for Rose to decide that James Cook—master mariner, voyager to the north Pacific, the Bering Sea, Tahiti, New Zealand and Hawaii, chartmaker for Newfoundland and the St. Lawrence River—had suffered from homesickness. His journals and letters reveal that he considered his real home to be 88

Assembly Row, Milesend, Essex, no matter how many years he was away at sea. Rose wondered if Cook had ever been reluctant to leave safe harbour in Lawn or the Nore or Spithead in England, or his Nootka Sound anchorage on the west coast of Vancouver Island, if he'd ever wished to stay longer in familiar ports the way she'd once wanted to stay in Prince Rupert, with or without Richard, instead of moving down to Vancouver.

In the morning, Rose looked down the hill path in the clear yellow Atlantic light, seeing that Lawn was as much a safe harbour from the wider, wilder Placentia Bay as Prince Rupert was a port of refuge from Hecate Strait. She had felt safe and lucky at home in Prince Rupert, but Eddie Rose from Newfoundland had been as empty and out of place there as she was in Lawn. Rose's Rock, one of the inshore trap fishing berths scattered around the bays and coves off Lawn Harbour, made her think of Eddie Rose. Grebe's Nest, Never Fail, Red Head and Old Man's Point, some of the berths are called. Bags of Bread, Pigeon Hole, Raggedy Rock, Pulpit Shoal and Rose's Rock.

Pages of Roses live in the eastern Newfoundland phone book in communities from St. John's to Lawn, but Eddie Rose was the only one in Prince Rupert. Eddie was an east coast trawl fisherman who lived one floor up from Richard and Rose in the apartment behind the Drifter Hotel when they first got to Prince Rupert. He was short, sturdy and generous. He brought bridge mix and green apples, although he didn't much like either of them, for the kids who lived in an attic across the street. Eddie drank a lot and didn't complain about anything, only laughed about how Rose would have doubled herself if she'd married him, and said once every week or so that he'd talked to one or another of the boys from home about getting a chance on a dragger working out of Prince Rupert.

Eddie pounded up the apartment stairs past Rose one day. He had to hurry, he called back, needed to pack his gear and get down to the boat. Hecate Strait and the Horseshoe, he said, then south for grey cod. If they got a good trip of fish, he might head out home for a while. Richard and Rose moved to the Beach Street house and she didn't see Eddie again. A long time later, at Carnegie Centre in Vancouver, she heard he was stabbed to death for his fishing cash in the alley behind the Princeton Hotel on Powell Street.

She left Lawn for St. John's on Slayney's taxi-bus, still keeping company with Eddie Rose in her mind, even if he might not have made it home to Newfoundland anyway, or maybe didn't know any more where he wanted home to be. Neither does Rose. She's only sure home isn't on the blue Pacific coast that knows she was ten years with Richard, almost as long married to the sea, and couldn't live up to either of them. Home isn't here in the unfamiliar Atlantic light either. But there are other places for vagrancy.

At first, in other countries, Rose can't be distinguished as a vagabond in exile. Perhaps in Minsk and Vitebsk and Pristina, all new world strangers are expected to possess a foolishly open countenance, as if the expansiveness of their still wild country is written on their faces, even stretched out in their long-legged steps. These visitors might well have living space in that other world, but their domiciles wouldn't be recognizable as home to anyone in the old countries. The ground in those North and South American places hasn't been tilled long enough. The rooms don't contain corners still holding the dry scent of grandmothers and their curtains, or the echo of older cousins' laughter.

But after a while wandering in the old world, Rose begins to lose the new. Her expression closes in on itself. Her footsteps shorten and she forgets to put on lip gloss most of the time. Sitting on park benches or in cheap cafés, reading Marina Tsvetayeva and Rilke and other poets who died before she was born, she looks up, startled to discover the oncoming end of the twentieth century. The poems could have been written last week. History lasts too long over here. The Danube/Dunav/Donau River runs too slowly, like the Vistula, the Moldau, the Drina and even the Volga. Rivers aren't expected to change things here, anymore. Not enough fireweed or kinnikinnik or heat-snapped lodgepole pine seeds come up to transform burned ground.

For a couple of years, Rose's aspect of absorption in a private world, and her tightly held pale mouth, create a woman who seems familiar to people in countries that were closed too long. Women and children and waiters anyway. Children in the Lublin train station ask incomprehensible questions, then stab the air impatiently with pale fingers, pointing to her father's pre-war Doxa watch. Kaliningrad women ask, probably, if the bus has already been and gone. Coffee waiters in Paris assume she is with the travellers offloading from the Bucharest tour bus and treat her with appropriate contempt.

Men in other places know Rose isn't from there because they're leaning across kitchen or café tables learning English from her. Private lessons for about ten Canadian dollars in dinars, rubles, levs, zlotys or korunas an hour. First English words: "Oh, my God," "haywire," and "moonshine." Enough students means enough money to eat and sleep in a small room near the train station. Not enough English students means long mornings in foreign banks getting hold of the made-at-sea money that has to last as long as exile, or long nights remembering to wear lip gloss while sliding slivovitz, scotch or bamboosh, the Adriatic summertime concoction of red wine and coke, across knife-scarred zinc countertops.

In Vienna, where no one needs an itinerant English teacher or bar maid, and where there's no cheap room near the train station, Rose calls her mother.

"Rosa...Rözchen, are you all right?" The voice in Vancouver is smaller and softer than Rose has ever heard it.

"Mama." The old name, not Canadian "Mum", or American "Mom", or a grown child's "Mother" but, "Mama, I'm fine. I'm in Vienna. Just for a day. It's expensive."

"Rosa, do you still have...."

Rose knows immediately what her mother means. "Yes, Mama, I'm wearing it right now." This is perhaps a forgivable lie. The damask linen camisole, with four American hundred-dollar bills and five twenties that her mother backstitched into the hem, lies in the bag crushed into the phone booth with Rose.

Backstitch, the strongest stitch used in plain hand sewing: working from right to left, take up six threads of the material onto the needle and draw it through; insert the needle two threads back from where it was last drawn out, and bring it through again six threads beyond.

Silence except for the sound of women breathing over the phone line from both sides of the world.

"Tell me the address. I want to go and look. I have all afternoon until the train," Rose says and anticipating the next question, "I bought a street map."

"I don't know the address any more. So long ago. Everything was all confusion and changing, even after the war." An attempt at the old sharp tone, "You can't imagine, Rose. Röslein." This is true. Overseas nomad or not, Rose is still planted deep in the new world. The leaves of Vienna's boulevard trees and the smooth-faced women in Jil Sander suits shopping on the other side of the glass phone booth tell her no more secrets about chaos and loss than Arbutus Street ever did.

"What street are you on?"

"Maria," Rose stumbles, "Strasse. Helfer. Hilfer. Mariahilfer Strasse." Mary's help street. Mother Mary who helps us street. Rose's mother's suppressed giggle escapes, runs wild into a gale of uncontrollable laughter.

"Go to the Kunsthistorisches. It's not so far. Toward Donaukanal."

Rose, after a suitable goodbye, a promise to write more

often and two glasses of red wine in the sun, consults her map and walks to the art history museum off Babenbergerstrasse. On display at the Kunsthistorisches is *Das Glass: der Beidermeyer, zeit Bohemia und Zuvot—Glass, Beidermeier*. Bohemia and Before.

Rose shuffles past pitchers commemorating Austro-Hungarian victories, then Venetian dragon-stemmed goblets and a handful of the glass beads Christopher Columbus carried to Hispaniola. She stop a while at a small Syrian mosque lamp, c. 1355 made of enamelled glass. The lamp's inscription is translated into English as well as German, *Gott sei Dank*: "God is the light of the heavens and the earth. His light is as a niche in which is a lamp, the lamp in a glass, the glass as it were a glittering star."

Swaying a little from sun and wine and no food, Rose still has centuries of museum glass to go. There's no sign here of the Queen of Sheba lifting her robe so as not to wet the hem while she stepped into what she thought was a pool of water in King Solomon's courtyard. "This is the palace floored with glass," Solomon told her while he admired her ankles in the mirror. The Celtic spirit messengers who come by sea in glass boats, and Arthur's soul, still alive in a glass castle on the isle of Avalon, are also missing from the exhibit. Rose stands long minutes before the last display, an eight-pointed star pendant, chipped, rough-surfaced, but still glass, made in northern Mesopotamia more than three thousand years ago. The glass star makes it possible for Rose to decide it isn't so far from Vienna to Mesopotamia, only long.

In Mespotamia the river had entered into her body, Rose thought afterward. She had felt the water slipping over the dry hills in her head, soaking into the desert lying dark between her ribs. She was still in Turkey then, but not not noticing anymore, only day dreaming out the windows of the bus belonging to the theatre company from Istanbul. The actors had found her at the hotel in Eregli the morning after their performance, sitting on the front steps beside her bags, looking as if she were watching a walnut tree, she supposed, but not seeing the tree and not thinking, "What next?" Without words, Abdullah and the Night Flower and the others knew this. They pointed to the window beside the double seat she could have to herself on their bus, and made soft bird sounds in Turkish until she got up and went with them.

On the bus, apricots were handed around, and paper cones of new almonds that squeaked between the teeth. There was tea in tulip-shaped glasses from stands by the side of the road in the long afternoons, and sometimes knife-cheeked government men who searched the bus and demanded papers. Rose floated in shallow daytime sleep with her head on the pillow provided by the ingenue who looked like blackberry pie, she thought, her flesh sweetly round and dark, her dimples and shining eyes glittering and winking like sugar on a baked crust. When the road swooped and curved and she opened her eyes, she saw the oval blue eye of Allah swinging in its small arc above the head of Mahmoud, the driver. *Inshallah* the eye whispered: *In God's hands*.

"Oh, easily. Where else?" Rose wrote in a notebook she

left behind in a field where they stopped to buy honey in the comb.

In the evenings, she sat behind dusty curtains in theatres in Tarsus and Mersin and other towns, waiting for the performance to be done, and dinner and sleep, keeping company with the wedding dress costume, the general's uniform, and the plastic pistol; befriending the military hats and skullcaps stacked in order of their appearance in the play, resting with her now beside a string of worry beads and a thick stage-prop book crowded among sugar-crusted tea glasses and Maltepe cigarette packets.

Three towns cancelled performances, and after Iskenderun, there was no dinner and no bed, only the bus loaded again, turning away from the coast. "To Diyarbakir, Inshallah," Abdullah muttered before he covered himself with a grey blanket and sank down in his seat across the aisle. The road unwound in the cooling night while the bus ran fast, whirling its content of soft Mediterranean air out doors and windows into a new sharp darkness. One light, another hour later, flickered and vanished far from the highway until the cool blue of a Turkpetrel station gleamed from a rise in the road. The bus engine sighed as it stopped and Mahmoud grunted softly, heaving himself from the driver's seat. Rose got off to sit beside him at a tea table inside the circle of fluorescence around the fuel pumps. Soiled white ducks prospected the asphalt at their feet while Mahmoud drank his tea and she looked up Diyarbakir in *The Lands of the Eastern Caliphate Mesopotamia, Persia and Central Asia from the Moslem Conquest to the time of Timur*, published in 1905. Nasir-i-Khusraw, the Persian pilgrim, passed through Diyarbakir in 438 (1046), and wrote a careful description of the city as he saw it.

The town was two thousand paces in length and in breadth, and its black stone walls surrounded the overlooking hill. In the centre of the town, a great spring of water, sufficient to turn five mills, gushed out; the water was excellent, and its overflow irrigated the neighbouring gardens. In the courtyard of the Friday mosque was a round stone basin, from the midst of which a brass jet sent up a column of clear water, which kept the level within the basin always the same. Near the mosque stood a great church, built of stone and paved with marble. Leading to its sanctuary, Nasir saw an iron gate of lattice-work so beautifully wrought that never had he seen the equal thereof.

The sanctuary gate's iron lattice had been shaped into tulips, Rose was certain. The marble on the floor of the eleventh-century church would surely have been cream coloured, threaded with green streams before the altar. People had thought the springs in the centre of town would water their gardens forever.

A truck without headlights screamed past the Turkpetrel station. Mahmoud stood and motioned to her to get back onto the bus. The sky was brightening now over a wide plain without people or villages, without wooden carts or Massey Ferguson tractors with blue beads strung around the exhaust pipes, where stones the size of a man's head were piled by the side of the road, and flocks of small brown birds flung themselves into the air as the bus passed. Rose set her pillow against the window and tried to sleep in the empty land, but she feared the dark behind her eyes. She sat up again and again, seeing only the stones and the startled birds until black walls rose matchbox height in the distance.

The highway broke into the basalt walls and Mahmoud stopped the bus before a narrow door marked Dicle Nehri Hotel. The actors went to their rooms and Rose walked down the street in Diyarbakir with *The Lands of the Eastern Caliphate.*

The walls of Diyarbakir were pierced by gates, namely the Water Gate, the Mountain Gate, the Bab-ar-Rum (the Greek Gate,) the Hill Gate and the Postern Gate (Bab-as-Sir, used in time of war.) In the seventh (thirteenth) century, Yakut speaks of the city as then covering a great half-circle of ground, surrounded by magnificent gardens.

The afternoon was half gone when she came upon the walls of the city again, to surrender beneath a stone arch deep enough to create a shadowed passageway, knowing she couldn't tell if this were the gate called Hill or Mountain or Water or War, and that she wouldn't find the iron flowered lattice leading to the sanctuary now. "Where is the museum?" she asked a tea boy, and the child set his tray at her feet and ran off, crying, "Aziz, Aziz, English!"

"The museum is forbidden now," Aziz said, thin and in his twenties, anxious under his smile.

Rose had forgotten English could be spoken in sentences. "Why forbidden?" she asked, meaning, "Is that so?" and "I don't believe you," and "It hardly matters."

"There is the house of a dead poet," Aziz said, watching her. "Also forbidden, but possible to see. A Kurdish poet." Aziz raised his hands in supplication to the guard who cracked open the door of the house along a dusty lane. His arms were slender, Rose saw, without enough flesh and muscle for a man. She passed him some lira for the guard and the door opened. The poet's home was arranged around a courtyard containing a plane tree, airy rooms lined with worn silk carpets and edged with cushioned benches and low tables. Between the shutters hung photos of a woman with deep pool eyes and bobbed hair, holding the arms of her daughters, helpful and serious on either side of their mother. The man who stood behind them, and alone in other pictures, turned his head from the camera, so that neither his eyes nor his expression were ever entirely clear. His desk was polished hardwood fitted with a multitude of drawers and brass-finished pigeonholes, all empty. Dozens of poems written with black ink in Turkish script on stiff cream paper had been framed and mounted on the wall behind the desk. Rose took *The Lands of the Eastern Caliphate* from her pocket and wrote a description of the desk and the framed poems on the front flyleaf.

Aziz stood in front of a portrait of the writer's shaded face, his head turned at the same angle as the man in the photograph. "This man was a secret poet, until he died and his poems were found," he told her.

"What was his name?" Rose asked.

"You are an artist also," Aziz said.

"What was his name?" Rose repeated.

"Writers and artists are shot sometimes in these days," Aziz said. "For security. The writers of newspapers and other things. Some people made a petrol fire for burning them. I don't know all the dead names." Aziz's words fell in fragments among the leaves of the plane tree whispering together outside the shutters. Rose listened hard to hear water running through his sentences over stone somewhere beyond the courtyard.

She made Aziz talk about himself on the way back along the lane, about how he was sometimes hired to work with the Shell Oil survey of the land between Diyarbakir and the Iraqi border; how the boss said all of his boys must try to work perfectly for the company, to make no measuring or drafting errors; about the thousand-year-old "caravanserai" where his uncle sold carpets, only foreigners didn't come to buy them any more.

"Let me take you to the play tonight," Rose said at the place where they had begun. Aziz's eyes widened, then his shoulders hunched and he made no reply. "Seven o'clock," she said, "Dicle Nehri Hotel," and she turned away from him.

The street was already dark, lit only with the tiny flames tended by men selling roasted hazelnuts from wheelbarrows, and by bigger fires burning rubbish on the pavement. Small boys gathered around these bonfires, laughing soundlessly as they poked each other and dodged away. They were eight and nine and ten, she thought, the same age she'd been when she saw her first fire out of doors at night. At summer church camp, she had stared into flames and no one had watched her or asked why. The counsellors told campfire stories about Artaban, the fourth wise man from the fabled east, the one who had dilly-dallied on his way to Bethlehem and missed the Christ child.

At twenty minutes to seven, Rose came out of the hotel to buy hazelnuts and found Aziz already pacing the street. His eyes were alight with excitement, she thought, but his mouth was set determinedly straight. He looked importunate, Rose decided, and she made him wait while she went around the corner to find a nut man. They didn't speak in the taxi to the theatre. Men with guns were at the door when they arrived, and Aziz hesitated, but she jerked his arm and pulled him inside, then left him in the lobby while she went backstage to collect their tickets. For the first time, she was to see the play from the audience.

When she returned to Aziz, more playgoers had gathered, but they stood apart from him. Two men in black suits were at his back and his face had gone still. She gave him his ticket and took hold of his arm, more gently now, feeling his body tremble, urging him towards their seats in the front row. Looking back, she saw that the men in black were gone, leaving behind them a sense of indrawn air, a space where they had stood that others still avoided.

Aziz's voice was cracked and dry, "I tell you they watch every moment that I am in this place. They are somewhere watching now."

The theatre was less than half-filled with people whose

faces were as smooth as the polished leather of their coats.
"Who are they?" Rose asked. "Government? Oil?"

"I have not come to this place before," Aziz answered.
"No one I know has come here."

Ah Biz Esekler, a voice announced. "We Are Donkeys,"
Aziz murmured. "A comedy." Abdullah appeared onstage,
small and fingering his worry beads exactly as he did in his
seat beside Rose on the bus, but more bewildered now,
ready to convince the audience that he was an ordinary
Turk, hopeful but confused about *demokrasi*. The blackberry
pie ingenue wore first a western-style wedding dress, then a
veiled chador; the general's glittering costume was on the big
man who usually helped Mahmoud carry the lights and
props; the Night Flower waved a schoolroom pointer; and
the actors used the thick book as a bureaucracy manual, then as
the Koran. All these presences whirled across the stage, tricking
and humiliating Abdullah's trusting little man. Beside
Rose, Aziz leaned forwards to catch each word of dialogue,
laughing soundlessly like the boys around the street fires.

"I did not know a play could be such truth as this," Aziz
whispered to her, making circumspect dancing motions of
his fingers in the direction of the stage. He didn't seem to
hear the repeated padded slap of the swing door as most of
the audience left the theatre.

The big man became a politician, babbling thunderous
words even Rose knew were not Turkish, just nonsense
syllables. Some nights he said "Canadadadadadacanada" to
make her laugh backstage. He was surrounded by the
young actors who sat at the back of the bus, transformed

into stage bodyguards who shoved the cheering Abdullah hard enough to make him fall.

"Ah, *demokrasi, demokrasi*," the entire cast sang at the end of the play. Aziz translated: "The prime minister changes, but nothing else is new. Don't be fooled by sugar *demokrasi....*"

"Sweet," Rose said. "Don't be fooled by sweet democracy."

"She's not for me and you," Aziz finished, his words suddenly loud in the silence as the curtains slid together and the actors vanished. Then the house lights came on immediately.

Aziz looked more boyish than ever, blinking in the electric glare, Rose thought, but the men in black hadn't shown themselves again, and she was hungry, afraid the actors would forget to take her with them to dinner. She stood up and shook Aziz's hand, cold and brittle in her grasp. "I must go." She waved toward the stage door.

"But you will return here?" he asked. She shook her head and left him crouched in his seat. She opened the stage door and stepped into darkness as it closed after her. Her hands moved forward, raising themselves to search the dark air. She half-turned to find the door again, to find Aziz and help him get home, to ask him to help her. Then the Night Flower's voice rippled out in a muffled flow, guiding her through the curtains in the wings into the every-night dismantling of the play. Only the haste and the absence of laughter were new. Mahmoud and the big man were rushing down the back stairs with the lights. The wedding dress and the other costumes already hung on their racks. Rose wandered among the actors and their props until she came to the familiar stack of hats, the worry beads, and the stage book. She carried them out to the bus and took her place. The streets were empty, lit only by Mahmoud's headlights. The bus stopped several times while Abdullah leaned from the window and answered questions from men Rose couldn't see. No one else spoke.

The restaurant will be bright, Rose thought. Everyone will talk and laugh again, and some of the dishes will smell like flowers. There might be lamb with yoghurt and mint, or the salad made from green olives, walnuts and pomegranates. The bus stopped at the hotel where lentil soup and rice gone cold waited in the twilight of the basement.

Wide awake in her room, Rose walked back and forth between the bed and the window. Diyarbakir was entirely still around her. She took out *The Lands of the Eastern Caliphate* and wrote on the back flyleaf:

1. Cancelled performances. Small audiences everywhere. Walkouts here.

2. Government men. Questions, rifles, black suits. Search bus. Guard theatres.

3. Television sets. None in Diyarbakir. Other places black and white, usually hotel desk or lobby. TV images seen: None. Not interested or fiddling with money. TV sounds heard: men's voices, neutral and explaining, or adamant and loud. Once in English (which town?) "There are not Kurds, only mountain Turks." Shots. Explosions. Keening, brief.

4. The forbidden museum.

5. *The dark streets.*
6. *Aziz. His words about writers and artists. Shot. Fire to burn them.*

She understood that Aziz might have gone home safely, and that she would not now, not in the morning, and not ever know for sure. Too tired to undress, or even to take off her jacket and boots, she lay down on the bed, but even with the overhead light on, the blanket beneath her became a dry field encompassing the width of her body, and stretching out on either side of her under a darkening sky.

At dawn, shrieking birds with wide, crooked wings came down on the field, and she ran to the window to escape them. Helicopters drifted above the heads of people in the streets. No one looked up into the scream of their engines. She sat down on the edge of the bed, and was still sitting there when the Night Flower came to find her, to put *The Lands of the Eastern Caliphate* into her bag and to lead her to the bus.

At the broken place in the black basalt walls, Mahmoud took the highway east to the mountains, not west to the coast. Rose didn't look out the window and she stayed in her seat when the bus stopped and the actors got out. The Night Flower and the blackberry ingenue stood in the aisle beside her. "Dicle Nehri," they said, and when she didn't move, they reached for her hands.

The Dicle Nehri Hotel might have drifted from its moorings in the city, then floated out to this dry ground, Rose told herself, but there was only a river running deep and fast over black stones. Abdullah handed her a piece of paper on which someone, the hotel clerk perhaps, had written in wavering capital letters DICLE NEHRI = BLACK ARROW = RIVER TIGRIS.

Rose stood at the edge of the bank and saw that the river water carried Aziz, still asking her if she would return, and herself, still shaking her head, no, and leaving him alone in the theatre. The Tigris carried the actors, blue gasoline flames, and the government men in black, along with Artaban, bearing his gift of a great pearl, seeing the men and women and children whose hunger caused him to hesitate, then to sell the pearl, to halt his journey under the distracting star again and again to give food and water and coins, each delay, he thought, moving Bethlehem farther beyond his reach.

For a second or two, Rose went back to Maple Grove school, where the Tigris River had decided to join the Euphrates and make a cradle to rock a rich, green land called Mesopotamia. She felt in her handbag for the weight of *The Lands of the Eastern Caliphate*.

Beyond the city lies the chief source of the Tigris, which Mukaddasi describes as flowing with a rush of green water out of a dark cave. At first, he says, the stream is small, and only of sufficient volume to turn a single millwheel; but many affluents soon join and swell the current. The beginning of the Tigris River, according to Yakut, was a distant two-and-a-half days' journey from Diyarbakir, and he, too, speaks of the dark cavern from which the waters of the Tigris gush forth.

After Diyarbakir, it's possible for Rose to cause a narrow green river of mercy and fruitfulness to flow past the windows of the Nokta Theatre bus on the road to Ankara. She is allowed now, too, for the first time in years, to remind herself that the Skeena River rises in the Gunanoot mountains where she has never been. A pilgrimage left undone in northwest British Columbia. For all Rose knows, the Skeena begins in Simon Gunanoot's mouth. She never even got to Graveyard Point on the bluff over Bowser Lake to pay homage to his bones.

Rose has travelled with Abdullah and the Night Flower, the blackberry pie ingenue, the big man and the boy actors, and all the characters they become every night on stage, longer than with any other company since the foreign fishing ships offshore. When the bus with dusty *Ah Biz Esekler* posters stuck on the sides turns out of Ankara toward Istanbul, she can't remember why she needed to leave the actors and go another way across Turkey. Their bags of farewell apricots and figs are in her hands. Their Maltepe cigarette and rosewater scent is in her skin. But if there is a river named *Dicle Nehri* for Black Arrow, there is also a Black Sea to be found, and then no way out of the port of Trabzon except back the way she came, or across the water. Rose never favours going back.

The passenger launch wallowed even at the dock in Trabzon, heavy with Russians and their disappointment, and the bags full of sun-faded clothes, scallop-edged silk buttons from another unimaginable century, badges on which Lenin's capped head was sewn slightly askew, flick knives and other goods they hadn't sold that day in the Turkish port. Halfway across the Black Sea, the crew locked the Russians, asleep or dead drunk by then, and Rose into a windowless passenger compartment. Hour after hour, a steep sea slammed the launch, sliding swollen bags shoulder high around Rose while her mouth dried, saying without sound or movement, "Let me out o god o stella maris star of the sea mother let me take off my silver whale bracelet and give it to the sea let me drown only let me out of this closed place."

In the night, a man with a hard brown, high-Caucasus face snapped a wooden match to light his way across a hill of baggage in front of her. There was the sound of water trickling from some hidden bulkhead tap into his tin cup, then secret movements within his wife's shawls as he struck another match and knelt to offer water to her and their child. Rose's eyes, pitlamped in the last sulphurous flare of matchlight, must have gleamed in the dark. The man lifted the cup in her direction, and when she nodded as the match went out, he leaned toward her, tilting the cup to her mouth so she could swallow sweet, earth-tasting water, then fall back into the cave of bags and sleep until the boat found a port in another country sometime before dawn.

The only photographs from Rose's time in that country are of bread and guns and tree stumps in black and white. Only two of these pictures have gone further than the contact sheets resting in plastic folders somewhere in the car parked at New Floats in Prince Rupert.

In that country, Rose crammed bread made without salt into her mouth while she ran in empty streets to reach locked doors, or stood by the side of the road trying to flag down one of the few vehicles still running. The cars jammed with passengers stuttered and stalled on bad gas. On haywire gas. Gas is always one of the first things to go, along with electricity, running water and heating fuel. Television and bread of one kind or another last longer. There is usually a faint smell of shit everywhere. Guns, pistols and long guns—automatic rifles, anti-tank weapons, and nineteenth-century single shot rifles with chased silver stocks—last until the end.

The money transaction was enacted with formality, despite the fact that Rose had to haul her underwear out of her bag while she knelt in the mud outside the car acting as the airfield waiting room. No need to deny the camisole's existence, or hide the hem ripping to find the dollars for a seat on an itinerant former Aeroflot jet. The plane's door didn't open, even then, until Rose had unfastened her small oval hoop earrings, 22K bright gold, the yellow gold the Russians, and mothers, like so much.

In the air, there was only a broken-armed seat, half a chunk of dark chocolate from a brigand across the aisle, and the one-note roar of jet engines into the night. There was a landing strip with a name Rose never learned, and train stations where she joined Russian, Ukranian and Belarussian communities living in silent villages built of bags on the station floors. After a long time, there was the pale, almost saltless Baltic Sea. But for Rose now, any sea will do. Any vessel will be a rescue ship.

Moving Water

*T*he cargo ship slowed to reduce its steep roll, steadying the Skeena River in Rose's dream. The engine noise under her pillow ground down to a lower note and she opened her eyes. The ship was Polish Ocean Lines' *M/S Tychy*, on the homeward passage of her Levant voyage, carrying containers from Gydnia on the Baltic to Casablanca, Alexandria, Beirut, the Syrian port of Al Ladhiqiyah, Hamburg, and back to Gydnia in thirty-five or forty days. The Greek islands lay out of sight off the starboard stern. Tunisia disappeared to port. Below Rose's cabin window, the amidships light glowed over the wooden picnic table on Deck 5, where the chief steward and his wife and the chief engineer waited for her on quieter nights in the early dark.

At the beginning of *Tychy*'s voyage, the chief engineer had been hidden behind the barricade of his work and his nightly bridge game with the motormen. He could be glimpsed carrying a flashlight and disappearing around companionway corners, stepping into the elevator to descend seven decks to the engine room, or sitting with his back to the door, playing cards in the crew's salon. He came on deck after the Baltic and the Great Belt to look at Skagen, the north-south turning point off the tip of Denmark. Halfway through the English Channel, he sent a motorman to say Rose could visit the engine room at 1000 the next day, if she wished, and drink coffee in his cabin's sitting room at 1030.

The chief engineer's English vocabulary seemed to be almost entirely technical while *Tychy* rounded from the open Atlantic to Casablanca. He spoke of fuel pumps, automatic ballast tanks, engine manoeuvres, pilot stations, cargo ramps and forklifts. Three days later, he explained his indignation at the captain's order to fire up the auxilliary engines so *Tychy* could make sixteen or seventeen knots to Alexandria once she passed the Straits of Gibraltar. With huge cupped hands, he gently placed imaginary auxilliaries alongside the main engines on his coffee table. He sketched all of his engines on a paper napkin, showing the auxilliaries gulping diesel and dollars, then drooping with fatigue. He prepared coffee for Rose in the mornings past Morocco, Algeria and Tunisia, and in the silt-brown harbour at Alexandria while *Tychy* waited for a pilot.

Before they left Gydnia, the chief engineer had seen Rose through the open windows of the aft cabin, sitting with her eyes closed and her head tilted back so the land breeze lifted the hair from her forehead. He knew she had no Polish grammar, only about one hundred words, which she spoke poorly, mixing Polish with Russian. She thought one of the sailors said the Moroccan coast before the Rif is supposed to look like a dead woman.

"Why dead?" she asked the chief engineer. Her first question. From the bridge deck, he showed her the breast hills, then the belly. Not dead, only pregnant.

Tychy bunkered in Beirut while Rose walked in the city. In the junk shop beyond the port gate, she found a small brass bell, waited while the shop's owner spun off its tarnish on his grinding wheel, paid him and went to the street tap he showed her so they could wash their hands together. But by the time Rose reached *Tychy*'s cargo deck, the bell sounded metallic and thin. Its note lasted too long in the air for her.

She left the bell beside the tin on the chief engineer's desk, and went to her cabin, refusing the rose-scented Nile tea she loved, as well as a chance to sit in the eye chair on the bridge while leaving harbour.

For the chief engineer, the bell brought back the cargo ship *Josef Conrad*: heeled over from American bombs at the river anchorage in Haiphong more than twenty years ago. He was third engineer on *Carina* then, in need of salvaging the *Conrad*'s engine room bell so he could be a hero on his own ship. Yet when *Josef Conrad* lurched on the changing tide, then began to fall, the rising floor of black water was familiar to him, even expected, as was the voyage his body made, swimming up ladders, reaching for lines drifting along companionways and finally pushing through to the surface of the water where *Josef Conrad*'s slanted deck had been.

During the ten-hour run between Beirut and Al Ladiqiyah in Syria, the chief engineer used some spoken

English as well as words underlined in his Polish-English dictionary and pictures drawn in pencil on graph paper to explain the twelve Polish girls who stowed away on the warships built in a Gydnia shipyard for the Indonesian navy in 1952.

"Dlaczego? Why?" Rose asked. "Why did the girls leave the place they knew to stow away for Indonesia?"

The chief engineer paused, probably to consider how to tailor the entire impossible truth of other lives to fit into the head of a woman drinking coffee more than forty years later, looking out the portside window as if the land and sea rushing past had nothing to do with her.

His steel ruler moved in a small arc above his desk. Maybe the sailors told them they would be princesses in Indonesia. But when the warships reached Jakarta—here the ruler snapped through the air—the Polish girls were out. Out.

Rose asked no more questions, said nothing of herself when she was a child or at any other time. She watched the Mediterranean beginning to pour toward the Strait of Gibraltar as if there was nothing else in her life. The chief engineer struggled with his dictionary to find the words to tell her that it is never wise to put to sea without strong memories of home port.

Tychy began her return voyage and the chief engineer opened the round tin on his desk. When the tin was new, it held hard candies from Wedel's Confectionery in Warsaw, then travelled four years on the chief engineer's first ship, a fishing trawler working the North Atlantic cod grounds, putting into St. John's, Newfoundland for supplies. The tin, gold-coloured and circled with a pattern of flowers and leaves flowing together on a black band, contained: half a dozen heavy needles stuck into a worn denim patch; coarse thread in black, white, brown and green; thumbtacks; five lightbulbs for Russian flashlights; straight pins and safety pins; seven plastic buttons, brittle with age, four white and three black; a graphite stick; two Grand Banks cod scales wrapped in a square of soft paper; a curtain ring from the cabin the third and fourth engineers shared on *Carina* and a chestnut from a tree on Malczewskiego Street in Bydgoszcz.

The chief engineer lived at Number Eight Malczewskiego Street in Bydgoszcz when he was ten years old. On March 5, 1955, his mother gave him five zlotys to take to the bakery two hundred metres along Malczewskiego for a loaf of the bread called *naleczowski*. He was running, he made Rose understand, for the pleasure of it when the siren sounded. Everyone around him stopped to stand silent on the street. He continued running. "Malchik, malchik," a woman called. "Hoch tutai." Boy, come here. He ran to her. Perhaps he bowed slightly. "Prosze, pani." Please, ma'am. She slapped his face one,two, three times. Our father is dead, she shouted, and held him by her side until the siren stopped, then pushed him away. He bought the bread and ran home to tell his mother. She trembled, he showed Rose, making his hands and body quiver, and said Stalin was not his father.

Jakarta, *M/S Carina,* the chief engineer wrote on a piece

of graph paper, pushing it over to Rose. Four Polish women walked up the *Carina*'s gangplank in Jakarta in the spring of 1973, he said. They wore stained sarongs and their hair was wrapped in rags. They lived in a whorehouse, they told the crew. Four of their companions from Gydnia were dead, four had disappeared. The chief engineer showed Rose how the women had put their hands together to pray, "Please captain, please, hide us and take us home." But the ship was guarded by Indonesian soldiers who watched everyone on board. The women wept. The captain, a good man named Guminski who'd been a naval captain in the Second World War, ordered the cooks to give them bread, kielbasa, cakes, oranges, apples, butter and tinned milk. The chief engineer feared the filth and running sores of the woman standing next to him in the companionway. The women, still weeping, left the ship with dunnage bags over their shoulders. At the foot of the gangplank, soldiers emptied the bags onto the dock and began to sort out what they wanted. The chief engineer started toward them, but they lifted their rifles and Captain Guminski ordered him back. No one on the ship saw the women again. The chief engineer had asked the woman he feared to tell him her name. Krystyna.

On the night *Tychy* was rolling toward the Strait of Gibraltar again, every slant of the ship splashed water from the edges of the six-stroke long saltwater pool beyond the picnic table on Deck Five. Rose knew the captain would order the pool to be drained tomorrow, in the Atlantic. She cracked open her door, and heard the chief engineer's deep laugh above Arab guitar music on the short-wave radio in his cabin. The door shut itself on the portside lean. She put on her bathing suit and ran down to the pool.

The water was only hip-deep by then. She lay on her back, arms curved over her head, legs stretched wide and let the motion of the sea and the ship and the pool move her body. The engines hummed in her ears below the surface. The sky was blacker than Pacific sky, the stars closer. *Tychy's* pitching increased, dumped more water out of the pool, swept Rose from one side to the other more urgently, pushed her under for an instant. The stars shone through saltwater. A warm shoulder touched her own. Billy Macken was there in the tiny, enclosed ocean of the pool, then standing below the stars, his smile half-hidden in the darkness past the decklights. The open sea, out of sight of land, makes you dream, awake or asleep, and then remember. Long offshore swells are best. If you stayed out there long enough, not talking much, you would remember everything.

Awash in the small sea rolling within a larger sea, Rose wept tears of relief into water as warm as new milk. She might have known Billy would find her if she waited for him in this watery cradle. The Bear Hunter is walking around the world here too, even if the North Star is lower in this sky.

Billy Macken sat down beside Rose's booth at the West End café in Prince Rupert late one Friday afternoon when she first worked on the Skeena River for Fisheries. She'd been climbing in and out of muddy creeks all day and still wore rolled-down hip waders. Billy persuaded the waitress to bring her a glass of wine instead of coffee, even though the West End didn't serve drinks without food.

Billy and Rose fitted into each other's shadows. His wildness subdued itself when he was with her. Hers, usually hidden from Richard and people at work, from anyone around her frequently, flourished. Rose satisfied Billy Macken's untended need to be a protector. Example: he was the one who remembered to go back to the bar for her hip waders after she took them off to dance that first night. And the next day, at the Bear Pass glacier outside of Stewart, Billy's hand, not Rose's, steadied the wheel when she laughed driving too close to the drop-off down to that grit-streaked ice. He didn't need protection, she thought, then.

Water in one form or another surrounded Billy and Rose. The glacier and the constricted ocean in Stewart Harbour near the head of Portland Canal, where British Columbia climbs up beside the Alaska Panhandle. The Skeena River along Highway 16, flowing down fast with the outgoing tides a hundred kilometres inland, running against them in the car upcountry to the Kitwanga turnoff, moving with them on the way back to the coast at Prince Rupert. At Meziadin Junction, where the Meziadin River meets the Nass, they always stopped at the fish ladder. Feeder creeks and tributary rivers accompanied all their roads. The creeks moved from mountain snows or ground-water streams, flowed out of forests and through meadows, joined unseen pools to lakes, dissolved into wider rivers, consumed by the Pacific between Stewart and Prince Rupert at the mouths of the Bear, the Nass, the Khutzeymateen and the Skeena. Even the American wine they drank was called Annie Greensprings.

Rose got back to Prince Rupert in time for work after the weekend she had met Billy and driven him home to Stewart. He disappeared, as he promised he would. At the end of the summer, Richard came home.

Once or twice a year for almost seven years, Billy appeared in Prince Rupert on his motor cycle. Rose never remembered its name, which disappointed him. He took her out on the bike every time he visited, driving sedately to the end of the green arched Skeena Slough road past Port Edward, and back to town. They never made love after that first summer. Billy was trying to get over lying, he said. But to her hands around his waist on the bike, he always felt the same, thin and warm. Every year, he asked if she still sometimes dreamed the running alone on the dry field dream. Some years, she said, "Yes." Some years, "Not so much."

"Run a river in that field," he said. But she didn't know what he meant, then. One year, Billy moved down to the south coast with a woman whose daughter was crazy about him, too. He came back the next spring. He never did get the trapline he wanted, instead he worked on geological expeditions in the mountains around Stewart, not as much as he would have liked. He wrecked his bike on the Dease Lake road, tore a cave in the muscles of his left arm. He missed a year's visits and sent back his Christmas card stamped "deceased." Rose smiled. Billy was up to something complicated. By spring, she was listening for his footsteps in the basement of the Fisheries building. Billy liked coming to find her safe at work, fooling around with photography on the side. He was always worried Fisheries would find out she still had the prints with Alert Bay pushed back into the forest, or underwater, as well as more recent photos of Ecstall River coho, handtinted gold, streaming into B.C. Packers' can warehouse. He never believed Fisheries wouldn't care.

Rose could easily have discovered for herself what had happened to Billy. She used to be good at finding out the news from friends, taxi drivers, fishery officers, commercial and sport fishermen, travellers, musicians, reporters, band councillors, mayors, beer drinkers, barkeepers, children, teachers and bootleggers in all of the country covered by the Department of Fisheries and Oceans' North Coast Division: north of Cape Caution to the Alaska border, including Haida Gwaii, the Queen Charlotte Islands; inland to the headwaters of the Nass and Skeena Rivers. She could have called the hotel where Billy drank, or the Sea-Alaska bar in Hyder, Alaska, over the U.S. border a couple of hundred metres along Portland Canal from Stewart. She could have called the post office or the RCMP.

Early in that last north coast summer, a man from Stewart brought Billy's story over to her table in the bar at the Rupert Hotel: Meziadin Lake and wine and an over-turned boat. Some girl faltering in the dark water and Billy going back for her.

Rose used to like details: exactly how the Fisheries officer's feet were placed in the creek when he first saw the bear; the jacket colours and middle names belonging to the seiners, trollers and gillnetters on the Skeena fishery management councils; the kind of pasta a girl she met at New Floats had eaten for dinner before she ran away from home; the brand name of the potato chips she saw a small boy steal from the store at Five Corners, then devour as if he were starving. But at the end of Billy's story, Rose didn't want details. She didn't want to know the temperature of the lake water, or who had been there the night he drowned, or what kind of wine they were drinking (Annie Greensprings?) or even where the grave was.

In the small spilling ocean on the Polish container ship *Tychy*, Billy's black hair, his half-memories of a mother long gone back to northern Saskatchewan; the time he got out of jail on a day pass in Prince George and there was no one awake to let him back in; the old denim jacket he found for her behind the Drifter Hotel, and all the ways she'd been careless when she knew him drifted through her, forward and back, from side to side, with the fluid angles of the sea. The air had cooled and the Bear Hunter stars had moved further from the ship.

The Bear Hunter lived long ago, when the Dene people and the animals were the only ones in the northern woods up the highway from the Kitwanga road to Stewart. The Bear Hunter was a young man, a little like Billy and Rose, maybe, restless and eager to move. One night he stepped from his lodge to look up at the sky and curse the Great Bear constellation for walking too slowly toward morning light and the start of the hunt.

The young man and his hunting dogs left the lodge at dawn, but the dogs became afraid and ran away on paths of their own, then the trail closed behind the hunter's footprints. He could only move forward alone, away from all that was familiar to him. In a clearing far into the forest, an old man waited, a man with white hair whose face was striped with vermilion. His voice was deep and strange when he said to the hunter, "You have cried out to the sky that I am too old and slow to walk across the night. Now, you will walk, and it will be long before you cover the ground between here and your home."

The old man gave the hunter a spruce wood walking stick with the power to find bears, and to show him the way when he was lost, but the spruce stick couldn't hurry the days or the seasons or the years of the Bear Hunter's journey across the world. His own hair was white and his steps were slow when he saw his home lodge again, small in the distance at first, then larger as he walked toward it, still grasping the spruce wood staff. The lodge roof was broken with snow. The house poles were grown over with moss. He set the walking stick into the ground at the lodge entrance, cleared leaves and pine needles away from his circle of fire stones, then made a fire and curved his body around the stones and slept. The night sky covered the roofless lodge and the sleeping hunter. Wind stirred his white hair and firelight striped his cheeks red while the Bear stars looked down on him.

When Rose lived up the coast, she loved the Bear Hunter's story because the hunter and the old man and the Bear stars changed shape with one another. Billy loved the story because the Bear Hunter came home at last.

The water left in *Tychy*'s swimming pool was only knee deep. A sailor stepped out from the bridge to switch on the stern deck lights. The Mediterranean still surged, but she wanted her tea and vodka with the chief engineer, and Billy was gone.

Tychy blacked out that night. A minor electrical failure, but the main engines stopped for five minutes, leaving the ship dead in the water, dark, and silent after the alarm bells stopped. When the chief engineer ran from his cabin to the stairs, he left Rose standing in the companionway at the edge of the circle of light from his torch, still holding her tea cup, listening to the heavy wash and fall of water along the hull. The sea noise receded as soon as they were under-way again, and she was gone when he returned to his cabin.

In the English Channel, when the slow rocking of the South Atlantic in fair weather had given way to a sharper coastal chop, Rose asked the chief engineer for graph paper. She sat hunched over the coffee table in his cabin, making him a map of the North Pacific coast because he has worked no further into that sea than the Gulf of Guyaquil and the Canal. For his information, she labeled channels, inlets, passages, capes, points, islands, rivers and villages north of the port of Vancouver and south of Anchorage. The names of these places, the names of their boats and people and animals and fish poured from her mouth.

That coast and its waters across the world hadn't been forgotten, only refused until other seas cradled Rose's body, lifting and falling, turning and pushing under her again.

In the River Elbe entrance to Hamburg, she pointed to an unnamed inlet on her map, put a star by the indentation, then made sharp mountains reaching down to the pencil lines of her coast. The star marked an old place, she explained. And in this place, she drew collapsing wooden houses almost covered by the forest. Bits of flowered dishes and blue glass beads mixed with the stones on the beach. The cliff in front of the houses is broken away, like this, she showed the chief engineer, shading layers of light and dark down the map's side, filling them with bone and shell fragments lying on beds of ancient ashes under the earth.

She looked out the open portside window at the flat land beyond the Elbe, watched her pencil roll down the table when *Tychy* took a broadside swell from the wake of an outbound Greek ore carrier. She examined the desk, telephones, lockers, and the engineer as if she were searching for the houses at the foot of the mountains, for the beach and the broken-away cliff, as if they should be waiting for her here.

The night before *Tychy* completed her voyage in Gydnia, the chief engineer took a needle and thread from the round tin so Rose could hem her skirt. He typed his engine pressure reports, stopping from time to time to watch her as she sewed.

Hemming is done by taking up the underneath layer of material at a distance of one thread from the hem, then inserting the needle through the upper layer, two threads above the fold at a slight slant.

The hem was finished when the chief engineer got up from his desk to sit across the table from Rose, turning the Beirut bell in his hands until it rang soft clear notes that caused her to believe she could manage Gydnia tomorrow, then more distant, Pacific harbours better known to her, and where she was known.

Memory is the truth about the one who remembers. Perhaps once she gathers her sewing and leaves his cabin for the last time, the chief engineer will begin to think that he knew her in St. John's almost thirty years ago. He might believe he can remember the night they walked together along the street with trees by the waterfront on their way back to the ship. On other occasions, he may forget that he has never seen the North Pacific coast.

"Carina," the chief engineer said when the hem was done. Beloved.

That last night on the cargo ship it was supposed to blow. They expected those steep lake-like Baltic waves. On the bridge, the captain and the radio officer talked about the *Estonia*, the ferry that went down between Tallinn and Helsinki a few years back. There was an argument about how many drowned. But the sea around them stayed quiet enough. The weather system had changed course and whirled away to Greenland. Wind, fair or foul, is only a possibility until it blows. On a boat, almost everything except an adjusted compass and a known point of land or star is only an imagined, hoped-for possibility needing to be proven every day of the voyage: the wind in the right quarter, the rigging ice-free and unsnapped, the sails still whole, the satellite navigation system accurate, the wood or steel or fibreglass hull still holding, the engines still beating, the nets full, or partly full, or back on board to try again, at least. Even ocean currents are only possibilities. El Nino, the warming sea named for the Christ Child, causes west-flowing southern Pacific currents to move east.

Rose turned down her bunk one last time and smoothed the flower-wreathed tridents woven into the worn white reaches of the damask sheets. The cargo ship sheets always smelled of ironing, and her own salt warmth, a scent Rose wouldn't have noticed if she hadn't seen Krystof, the steward, burying his face in her dirty linen on laundry day after Beirut. He gave permission for one sheet to leave the ship with her. It could be made into a night-gown or a shirt, Rose thought, if she ever saw a sewing machine again.

When the ship still moved under her body on the last night of the voyage, rolling delicately, then more deeply as their course shifted, Rose began to believe there might be comfort in the ambiguity of the past as well as the future. She could have given birth. Richard and the child would have been safe from her if she had found mercy to give herself as well as them. Billy Macken might, in time, have expected more than wildness from her. She might have returned the favour. These former possibilities were never forbidden, she thought, only lost.

The chief engineer probably had chances yet to come to be more, or other, than the man he already was. His wife, he said, saw him as a safely enigmatic pirate, sailing seven unimaginable seas, appearing inland occasionally at home in Torun with his loot. Rose knew him to be a man who husbanded his huge diesel engines, and the itinerant souls in his care—from the young motormen and the nervous second engineer to her—with the sturdy devotion of a soldier monk. By day, he wedged the shaded portholes in his cabin so the brightness bouncing from the sea shimmered as drops of light around her At night in the chief engineer's cabin, the lamps on their chains swung with the sway of the ship, brushing soft yellow light over them. In his cabin, she had the chance to be almost beautiful. Even after the ship, standing on the asphalt dock in Gydnia, with the portal of *Tychy*'s huge roll-on, roll-off container deck at her back, Rose could imagine that she still held possibilities other than restlessness and vagrancy.

My bonny lies over the ocean
My bonny lies over the sea
My bonny lies over the ocean
Bring back my bonny to me
Soon there'll be no difference between the land and the water
I can walk on ice to places I've never been
When I get as far as I can go I'm gonna turn
And throw my cares over my shoulder
Along with your memory
Just let it all float down the Gulf Stream
And I'll walk home singing
My bonny lies over the ocean
My bonny lies over the sea
C'mon bring back, bring back my bonny to me
    —traditional song wiith additional lyrics by
    Laura Smith

On Roberson Point

*E*nding a journey with no meaning beyond itself required other journeys, each one issuing into the next, with necessary renunciations between them. The distance from Gydnia to Warsaw needed Rose to forgive the weight of land around her. In Warsaw, the post office on Swietokrzyska Street arranged another voyage, but only for the boxes of contact sheets and film marked "sea mail," which arrived safely on Arbutus Street two months after she'd flown back to Vancouver. Air Canada supplied an unbroken seat, and a seat belt.

The house on Arbutus Street had become an island with a softened shoreline, a place where Rose and her mother, as best they could, were kind to each other. Rose's mother called her Rosa sometimes, and asked her to make tea for her in the evenings. She didn't want to sell the house, she said, even if it was too big for her now, because the *Floribunda* rose, unaccountably, without care, still blooms every year.

Sitting at her dining room table, still in its place by the side window, Rose's mother watched her arrange the first prints from the sea mail packages to form a body lying on the polished mahogany surface. At the top, a stone the size of a man's head, cropped from a photograph of the road back from Diyarbakir. In place of arms and legs, stumps of plane trees cut down from the boulevards of Tbilisi for firewood after heating fuel and coal ran out. Joining head and limbs as the torso of the figure, a river, running high in spring flood, photographed through the dusty window of a bus driving through the Mur Valley in eastern Austria.

Rose's mother looked a long while in silence at the body made from parts of other countries resting on her table. "Tell me how it was before here," Rose said to her. "I want to understand."

"You can't understand, Rozchen. You are from here." But she got up from the dining room table and brought Rose a photograph of a young couple, snapped in mid stride by the street photographer on Granville in downtown Vancouver in 1954. The woman wears a close-fitting soft hat with scalloped edges. Her mouth, surprisingly full and lipsticked dark, is slightly open. She must be saying something to the young man whose arm she holds. He leans towards the flower face turned up to him, but his gaze seems to slide past her to survey the street around them. A tightly held sharpness evident even in his slightly too-large dark suit, and the same tension in the angle of the woman's head and the clutch of her hand on his sleeve seems to say, "Be wary," even here, in this new world.

In the space of a breath, Rose saw the possibilities. Her *Women in Glass Vessels* could contain two versions of this couple who hoped crossing the sea to the other side of the world would be transformation enough. The first, an exact copy of the original photograph, with black photo corners stuck into the edge of a mirror. The second, blown up to at least ten by fourteen, maybe matted with gold foil, and hand tinted. The faces will remain pale. Her mother's mouth will be reddened. Her father's too-dark eyes will be brushed with a touch of the light as when he looked at his roses, and sometimes at Rose. It may be possible to cover both prints with stained glass of the same persistent yellow gleam as a pale winter sun.

One night, Rose's mother asked her, "Why do you like it up there in that stony place?" She waved in the direction she meant to be northwest.

It was Rose's turn for silence. "It's a comfort to me," Rose said at last. "And the water." Her hands curved into tentative, rippling motions. Her mother nodded.

She gave Rose her car. "Take it," she said. "It waits for you all this time." It was possible then, in a car crowded with glass wrapped in her mother's oldest blankets, to go back the way she had come fourteen years before. From Georgia Strait up the coast, the sea was quiet for October, only licking and lapping the ferry hulls and the hard-bitten beach. Barret Rock was there on the starboard side when the *Queen of the North* entered Prince Rupert harbour. In the morning, Rose found a place to light for a while until she got some kind of job. Two rooms, one for sleeping, one for working on prints and the glass pieces. Both rooms gave her a corner glimpse of the water.

When someone departs he must throw his hat,
filled with the mussels he spent the summer
gathering, in the sea
and sail off with his hair in the wind,
he must hurl the table,
set for his love, in the sea,
he must pour the wine,
left in his glass, into the sea,
he must give his bread to the fish
and mix a drop of his blood with the sea,
he must drive his knife deep into the waves
and sink his shoes,
heart, anchor and cross,
and sail off with his hair in the wind.
Then he will return.
When?
Do not ask.

— Ingeborg Bachmann, *Songs From an Island*

The woman who returned from heaven to fall into stone on Roberson Point is far from the sea's reach now. The tide in Venn Passage has retreated to full stop at low-water slack. About fifteen minutes more still water until the tide starts its six hour climb to high before midnight. All winter, the highest tides here will lip the petroglyph woman again and again, filling her head and body with still water. The edges of the *Woman Who Fell From Heaven* are wearing under this wash, and rain and storm wrack. In time, a long time, she'll dissolve into the sea again and move within it.

When I worked for the Fisheries up here, when I was still married, I lay in the bath one night on Beach Street, shifting my shoulders up and down so the water moved around me.

"You always do that," Richard said.

"Do I?" I asked him. "Do I?"

Moving water must be the first memory. The green glass float that will be filled with seawater bearing the small figures of the petroglyph woman in black resin, and me, made of bird bone, could be called *Before Birth*.

The tide will turn toward the petroglyph woman again about six minutes from now. There's no need to hope for this to happen. It will. There is that comfort.

Only human beings and their stories need hope and its possibilities. Hope was all Psyche had to go on after she lost Cupid. "Wandering day and night, without food or repose," she found means to prove her repentence for being suspicious of love by sorting Venus' seed grains, then entering a certain cave to find the black river to the underworld. Charon, the ferryman, had the grace to allow her to return the way she had come.

If Psyche could restore her loss, maybe the Metlakatla girl who mourned her nighttime husband found an ordinary man not carrying so huge a secret between night and day. Maybe she bore children, easy boys, and at least one daughter who was more difficult, who was too much like her mother, and not enough, who was restless and a stranger and dearly loved, all at once.

In a moment or two, the indrawn breath between the tides will pour out to push the sea into the rhythm of its rise. This watch is almost done. Time will begin to move again, as it does when a sandglass is turned. These sandglasses were still used on ships until clocks tolerant of unceasing motion were developed. In this old means of measuring time in the wheelhouse, the sand in the upper vacuum globe empties itself through a narrow neck in half a minute, half hour, one hour or four hours. Only when the glass is clear has the watch time advanced. Only when the sandglass is reversed can the measurement of your time begin again.

To clear and turn my own glass of time already gone, I need to be here on the hard coast that knows me and still offers consolation. Here I can imagine art and other ways of moving and changing course and overflowing the banks, even if I stay in one place. This is all I know about being Rose, Rosa, Rosie, Wild Rose Bachmann, anymore.

It's almost dark now, and raining again, but Richard will come around the Point any moment with his skiff and his sons. His mouth will be set tight to conceal his response to salmon who didn't return from the sea, and a woman who forgot how much easier it is to get off Roberson Point at high water, or at least mid tide.

He still won't step onto the beach here, but the boys will. They may only glance at the full-length petroglyph figure behind me, being more interested in getting me and my bag over the rocks and into the skiff so they can cheerfully battle each other for the wheel once Richard has us into the

Pass again. The city of Prince Rupert will be an assembly of lighthouses in the early dark, and the boys' mother will be waiting for us at New Floats. She is Grace, from the Nass, who lives up to her name and who is not disturbed, or perhaps much interested, by me.

In the skiff, I'll reach out into the spray flying past us, and see the water streaming off my hands like liquid glass. Glass was discovered by sailors, Pliny says, more than three thousand years ago. They beached their boat and built a fire to cook supper, using a block of natron, an alkali they were carrying as cargo, to prop the cooking pot. The sand under the fire melted and moved in a stream that hardened into a new, translucent, light-bearing substance.

I want to learn to pour glass. Because the recipe is almost the same today as it was given on a cuneiform tablet in the seventh century before Christ: sand, ash or another alkali, lime and fire. Because it runs like a river and then cools clear. Because it lasts until it shatters, and can be remade.

ACKNOWLEDGEMENTS

I am grateful for help from Mildred Roberts, Ed Spalding and the Spalding family of Gitsumgalum, Terrace, B.C. and from Mary and Bill Kelly of Lawn, Newfoundland; the Department of Fisheries and Oceans, Pacific Region, North and South Coast Divisions and the Institute of Ocean Sciences; the Canadian Coast Guard, Pacific Region, French Creek Station; and Prince Rupert City and Regional Archives. I would also like to thank Edna Alford at the Banff Centre's Writing Studio who suggested that the landscape that Billy and Rose travelled was large enough for a novel.

Books important to my research include: *Images of Stone B.C. Thirty Centuries of Northwest Coast Indian Sculpture* by Wilson Duff (Hancock House, 1975); *Pacific Fishes of Canada* by J. L. Hart (Fisheries Research Board of Canada, 1973); *Crossroads of Continents: Cultures of Siberia and Alaska* (Smithsonian Institution, 1988); and *The Penguin Dictionary of Saints* (Penguin Books Ltd., 1965). The book Rose consults in Diyarbakir is *The Lands of the Eastern Caliphate: Mesopotamia, Persia and Central Asia from the Moslem Conquest to the Time of Timur* by G. Le Strange (Frank Cass and Co. Ltd. by arrangement with Cambridge University Press, 1966). The story of Psyche and Cupid is from *Bulfinch's Mythology* (Avenel Books, 1978).

Permission for use of the following material is gratefully acknowledged: "Freshes" from *The Oxford Companion to*

Ships and the Sea, edited by Peter Kemp (Oxford University Press, 1976); the excerpt from *The Crying of Lot 49* by Thomas Pynchon (Harper & Row, 1980); "I thank you, Lord" and "I've opened my veins" from *Marina Tsvetayeva Selected Poems*, translated by David McDuff (Bloodaxe Books, 1987); "Cedar Rain" by Ken Hamm from *Eagle Rock Road* (North Track and Malahat Mountain Music, 1995); "My Bonny" traditional song with additional lyrics by Laura Smith from *b'tween the earth and my soul* (Cornermuse Recordings, 1994); and "Songs from an Island" from *In the Storm of Roses: Selected Poems of Ingeborg Bachmann*, translated, edited and introduced by Mark Anderson (Princeton University Press, 1986).

Portions of this work have been previously published in different forms in *Prairie Fire, Journey Anthology (1993), Border Crossings, West Coast Review, Grain, Westcoast Fisherman* and *Left Bank*. Earlier versions of some parts of the book have been broadcast on several CBC Radio programs including "Ideas" and "Gabereau."